Pandora's Box

Jenny hadn't even bothered to unpack her traveling case. It lay open on a chair, spilling hose, costume jewelry, a lace nightie.

Years of picking up after her sister made Laura react automatically. She reached out to straighten the things and close the case, but something held the lid open. She took out a pair of shoes . . . and stared down at a bundle of green printed paper bound by a thick rubber band.

Laura picked it up, turned it over with a growing sense of unreality. It was money. Bills. Fifties, hundreds . . . there must be four or five thousand dollars.

Dazed, she never knew Jenny had come up behind her until she heard a flat, frightened voice say: *"What are you doing snooping in my things?"*

PUT PLEASURE IN YOUR READING
Larger type makes the difference
This EASY EYE Edition is set in large, clear type—at least 30 percent larger than usual. It is printed on scientifically tinted non-glare paper for better contrast and less eyestrain.

Laura's Island
Mary Vincent Hunt

VALENTINE BOOKS,
NEW YORK

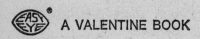 A VALENTINE BOOK

LAURA'S ISLAND

Valentine Books are published by
LANCER BOOKS, INC., 1560 BROADWAY
NEW YORK, N.Y. 10036

Chapter One

When she was still a hundred yards from the rotting pier, Laura Brown cut the switch on her red outboard and let herself drift in toward the shadowy point.

Strange, she thought again. *Very strange.* But strain as she would, she couldn't catch the faintest sound of it now.

A flight of birds homed noisily across the sunset, feathering down to rest on the dark island ahead of her. Waves lapped against the boat's side like a faint tattoo of warning. Even her stillness carried its own murmurs. But that other sound— that strange, lost rhythmic thing, partly music, partly just a beat—was nowhere.

Could I have imagined it? Hardly! Laura told herself.

Three times during this past week, as she criss-crossed the lake to teach the various swim groups she held for the resorters' children, she had heard it coming from the island. Yet who could be playing? Who *could* play like that? And on what?

The problem of identification alone annoyed her. Her record collection back at her cabin was selective—it had to be when often the choice was between a longed-for recording and the day's groceries—but no jazz artist and no instrument she had ever heard had been able to give off such a thin fire of sound, falling away into that hollow beat.

Besides, the island itself—Spider Island, the "natives" like herself still called it—was deserted. All that remained of some ancient summer were the shambles of the pier ahead and the burned-out shell of a cottage.

Even when her father, Lee Brown, had owned Spider Island, along with the old Lee's Landing, which had once sprawled across the north shore, people had avoided it, distrusting a shore line that offered either muck up to the neck or depths that had never been sounded. Now that all Talisman Lake had changed so radically since those remote years of a difficult childhood—becoming ringed with exclusive lodges and resorts—no one was tempted to build on Spider Island.

Not that I'd let anyone, Laura thought.

Perhaps her sense of love and possessiveness was a bit fierce, but so little remained since Lee Brown's death almost ten years ago. All she had managed to salvage were the old house in nearby Lakeville, which still sheltered her winters, the cabin on the north point beyond the newly risen Lee's Landing, and the strangely menacing island that still comforted her heart.

Even Jenny had vanished. Three years ago this very summer.

6

Jenny of the silk-gold hair and the incredible beauty, three years younger than the sometimes-discouraged sister who was close to twenty-three, and centuries more knowledgeable.

Had Jenny found whatever she craved? Laura often wondered. The man, the career, the ambition? Or was she still burning herself out, living for the moment?

It was difficult to keep from being drawn into that aching train of thought that always ended on the same note of loss, the same weight of responsibility. Plagued by memories of their too-lazy childhood, Laura had held a thousand debates with herself on the subject of failure. How much more should she have done, could she have done, for a sister like Jenny?

Even Laura had forgotten what their mother had been like. But she had not forgotten Lee Brown—that charming but quixotic father who had thrived on running his third-rate summer resort, only to hibernate in gloom through the snowy winters in town while his daughters got on with their schooling.

They'd had some attention from various house-keepers, Laura remembered, plus another kind of education from the old-time resorters who rattled up from Chicago in their cheap cars—those flashy women with the loud voices; the men who were always ready with the wink and the inviting smile.

How she had detested those men. Unfortunately, she was forced to admit, they'd had some provocation, since both her father's daughters had been plagued with the kind of beauty that picked up trouble like radar.

Early and expertly, Jenny had learned how to handle hers, but Laura had gone on the defensive, withdrawing herself as much as possible, welcoming the lonely security of the lake itself, the woods, the hours when she could fish alone, or swim, or escape to her deserted island, so perilous with dream—

Abruptly, Laura's reverie was splintered.

Her motorboat had nudged the ancient pier, splintering another piling, and she was left with the practical matter of deciding whether to tie up and risk a scramble over the rotten boards and a possible fall into muck as dangerous as quicksand, or to forget the whole thing.

Forget it, she decided. If someone was trespassing, ordering them off would be unpleasant. Besides that, she wasn't dressed for a lonely encounter with a stranger. Both her beach towel and jacket had been used to wrap up a pair of shivering six-year-olds after their last lesson, reducing their teacher to a serviceable white swim-suit, plus a pair of sneakers with twice-broken laces.

But just as she reached out to shove off, that playing started again, catching her under the heart—those fire-thin notes across that blue and aching beat!

Like some mystic harping, it lured her onto shore, leading her into a hard struggle with the lower thicknesses of scrub oak and dogwood. The path—there was no path—led upward, and when she reached the freedom of space again, she was on the cliff, breathing hard from the climb.

This high ledge of rock where she had played as a child—risking the long swim out just to have it for herself, Queen of a Watery Domain—was still the same except that a cut of rock had crumbled away, exposing a treacherous drop to water chilled to an unknown depth.

Separated from her by that crumbled-away chasm, sitting here on a large stone, so stupidly near the edge, was a man. An absorbed, bony-thin man with rough red hair and bent shoulders and a cradled guitar.

But a guitar!

How could it be; the sounds he was drawing from it—Yet it was. And even as her attention fastened itself nervously on his precarious perch, the rest of her half-stunned mind was searching for a comparison evoked by his playing.

The Spanish guitarists? The great ones? His artistry was as American as the blues, as tight as a jet. And only an authentic genius could sit there in a trance on the edge of nothing an make rock-'n'-roll sound as intricately inspired as Bach!

Suddenly his playing snapped off. Her foot had slipped on the bare stone, dislodging a cascade of pebbles, and he had jerked around, searching for the sound.

She had never been stared at—or through—so

9

strangely. She might have been plain, or old, or ugly. Or not there at all.

"I'm terribly sorry! I didn't mean to startle you," she called to him.

She watched his shoulders bend again, the alertness wash out of his face. He had a sulky mouth and a vulnerable jaw, and he needed a haircut. He looked tired too. And she couldn't quite decide why she instantly liked him so much.

He said, "That's O.K. I startle pretty easy these days."

Frozen, Laura saw him stand up with a vast clumsiness, shift his guitar, and fumble through his pockets. Another six-inch step and he'd be over the edge. If the pebbles slipped under him, he'd be over right now. With a feeling of explosive impatience she watched him fasten the black glasses across his eyes. And then she realized he was blind.

The silence thickened, and there began to creep up on her that distracted sense of responsibility toward anything lost or wounded or helpless. She didn't how how to start—with an apology or a warning.

"Won't you please sit down again?" she said at last. "A crevice has broken away right at your feet, and it might be rather a nasty drop. I'll tell you—you sit down and I'll come up from the other side of the cliff and"—she did not want to sound as though she pitied him—"and we'll talk."

Blind and alone on Spider Island! she exclaimed to herself as she plunged back down through the underbrush. But he could hardly be alone, she realized angrily. Some extremely irresponsible companion must have let him wander into such danger. The red-haired guitarist might well resent having his disability fussed over, but this was almost criminal neglect.

Both anger and urgency made her claw at the bushes that held her back. A talent like his was special. And up to now, she had met few men whose eyes hadn't betrayed an instant physical response the moment they saw her. It would be strange indeed—and rather a relief—to be able to talk to a man who couldn't see her at all . . .

There had been a path once, circling the point to the other sie, but Laura couldn't immediately find it. Everything seemed to conspire against her. Thickets held her back and vines snared her feet. Stifling a yelp of pain, she was forced to stop dead and try to free her long black hair from a twisted branch. It was still damp from her last swimming lesson, and she should have pinned it up. Now it held her by the roots.

It was a bad moment to be startled by a man's voice. Curt as a guard, somebody behind her said, "Take it easy. You won't look so good scalped."

Another stranger? Another trespasser on Spider Island? she thought. The traffic was getting heavy. But fear was jamming at her, too. This one didn't sound friendly. Still ensnarled, she had to twist to see him, tears of pain distorting her vision.

11

His shirt was a blur of white in the green gloom. It seemed to come at her with a tight and impatient movement, but when she felt his fingers in her hair, they were careful. And surprisingly gentle.

It took him several minutes to free her.

Once he said gruffly, "I'm sorry. I'm trying not to yank it." He stood very close, but she knew he had to. She tried to mutter at him, but that only increased her embarrassment. She felt something strain between them—something more difficult to endure than having to stand quietly while he hurt her like this.

"Thanks!" she gasped, able to move away from him at last. "That was awful! I was hurrying"— her breath caught—"I mean, I have to hurry!"

"You don't now," he said, and deliberately barred her way.

She didn't try to step past him. Dark, and square of jaw and shoulder, he carried an attitude that momentarily confused her. He seemed withdrawn and preoccupied and just a shade antagonistic. The antagonism was probably unconscious on his part, she realized—that spontaneous flicker of distrust that she had encountered with many men. Men seemed able to forgive cross eyes or bowlegs, but sheer beauty in a girl was somehow a dishonest trick she was playing on them.

"Please," she said sharply, "there's someone up on the cliff—"

"Not now there isn't."

"Then he's fallen. He must have! He was right on the edge, and he's blind."

But this man wasn't. His dark gaze had already inventoried her assets, and there was a look coming over his face that unsettled her even more—a shadow of perplexity and wonder in the eyes, a tight line of refusal on the mouth.

She was about to let her mouth snap open when he offered a curt explanation.

"Burny's safe," he said. "As a matter of fact, he isn't completely blind. I mean, he can see lights and shadows sometimes, and he likes to get around without any help. But he told me what happened, and he thought I'd better find you."

"Why?"

"To thank you."

"It was nothing."

"You do it every day, I suppose."

He made her nervous, and she shrugged impatiently, but she felt an inner sag of relief, of thankfulness that Burny was safe.

Burny? she wondered. Was that his real name? Perhaps he had acquired it because of his red hair or the way he played that devilish guitar. But it didn't matter; he was safe. And it was late. If she didn't hurry, it would be pitch dark before she could get back across the lake.

"I was wondering—" said the man with the level gaze. "Will you come back to camp and let Burny thank you himself?"

"That isn't necessary."

13

"But it might help."

"Help whom?"

"Help Burny," he told her impatiently. "Let's put it this way. Burny wouldn't have cared too much if he had slipped over the edge. Three months ago he had an—accident. The doctors insist he ought to be getting his sight back, but he isn't. Psychological blindness, they call it. They say he can't see because he doesn't want to see. Well, he's got his reasons. He's a good guy and a great musician, but he can't get with it any more. Won't even work. So I thought a change might help. The outdoor life where things aren't complicated. Maybe even a few easy gigs around the lake."

"Gigs?"

"A playing date. Music. One night only."

"I see. So you brought him here. You wanted gigs, so you picked a deserted island in the center of the lake. Why didn't you try outer space?"

"Because our cash is running short, and this place is for free. At least nobody's been around yet to collect the rent. Besides"—his voice narrowed—"I figure if we can just stick around here for a while, we may run into an old friend who could help Burny."

"*Here*? Don't be silly."

"I'm not. For a few seconds I thought you were her."

She considered whether to inform him that she was the owner of Spider Island, but then he might insist on paying her that rent they couldn't afford. So she said instead, "Nobody comes to this island. It's been deserted for years."

"What are you? A castaway from a beauty contest?"

"I'm the local swimming instructor. And I happen to work in this outfit!"

"Some work." But he caught her arm. "Wait a minute. I'm sorry. This scare over Burny got me rattled, I guess. And you—well—"

"Afraid to say it? I bother you. I've been bothering people since I was thirteen. But I'm a small-town girl with very narrow principles. I have no ambition to be different, no major problems. I'll go along with you simply because I'd like to help your friend. So relax."

But he didn't relax. As he trudged ahead of her through the woods—still without a name to match those wonderful shoulders—the back of his neck remained as stiff as his attitude, and he strung a silence between them that began to irk her.

Was he naturally difficult and suspicious, or did he blame himself in some way for his friend's blindness? A layer of guilt could account for such curtness. Then again, this kind of reaction in a man wasn't new to her. Back when her younger sister was still at Lee's Landing, Jenny had pinpointed it once for her.

"Men," Jenny had said contemptuously, surveying her face in a mirror after a date. "If a girl happens to have something special, they either flip right away or try to cover it up with meanness. Or they get superior. How I love to make them jealous, then laugh."

"Jenny!"

"Oh, stop being a square. Face it. How many men treat you naturally? The way they treat other girls."

"I'm not interested in 'many men,' " Laura had said testily.

"Well, I am! And someday I'm going to leave this Hicksville and find one who's rich enough to appreciate me. Believe me, if I can just find him, I can marry him, too."

Poor Jenny. But she had made a point. Few men did seem able to treat her casually, Laura had to admit as she kicked a log out of the way. Perhaps that accounted for her own stand-offishness. But suddenly her gaze searched for the man ahead of her, then lingered.

She really should have ordered both him and his blind friend off the island. But the moment of choice had passed. Both of them had already begun trespassing on areas of uncertain emotion, she realized. Was it pity? Liking? Curiosity?

Laura's heart seemed to lag as uncertainly as did her feet on the pathway. But what sobered her to a sudden standstill was the strange little pang that shot through her when she looked again at the man in front of her—a pang sweet and tremulous and aching. Totally unlike anything she had ever known before.

Chapter Two

The man with the white shirt and the difficult attitude led Laura on around the cliff and then down the overgrown shore line until they came to a cove that she remembered well, even in the seeping dusk.

It was a good spot for a camp, cuffed by one of the few strips of safe and sandy beach on the island.

A rowboat had been drawn up into the reeds that laced the turquoise gleam of Talisman Lake, and a pot of coffee steamed on the camp stove. Her gaze went on to inventory some folding chairs, two sleeping bags, and a table with two gasoline lamps—inexpensive rented equipment, from the looks of it.

One of the lamps was lighted—a beacon for frantic moths—and down on his knees in front of the other lamp, awkwardly fumbling with a matchbox, knelt the blind guitarist.

For just an instant as it caught, a match pinpointed twin flares in those pitiful black glasses, before it burned his thumb and he muttered helplessly, "Blast it!" then started the operation all over again, only to jerk up his head at the sound of approaching footsteps.

"Easy, kid. It's only me," his friend said. "What are you trying to do? Fry us some fingers?"

"The boy-scout bit. I don't dig it. Take over here, will you, man, before I blow myself up."

Even when Burny stood up, he seemed to sag. But after he had felt around beside the table for his guitar and slung it up against him, Laura could sense his relief. It was hard to tell which was supporting the other—man or instrument.

A glitter of aimless blue notes seemed to spill out at his bare touch. "Did you find her?" he asked.

"I brought her back with me. I thought maybe—"

"He thought I'd like to meet you formally," Laura broke in. "And I certainly would. I hope you don't mind."

"Who minds? It's my pleasure. I don't get my neck saved every day." He plucked out a listless rhythm, and his square-jawed friend gave Laura a look of appeal.

"I wasn't too much interested in your neck," she said. "Just your music. I think it's wonderful. Honestly. That's what lured me up to the cliff. I've got a pretty good record library, but I've never heard such a beat. When I first heard you, I couldn't believe it was coming from a guitar. Then I thought, if Andres Segovia were to play some sort of jazz written by Bach—" She spread her

18

hands helplessly and laughed. "But even that wouldn't sound like you."

"Dig her. I should hope not. I'm just a mortal." But Laura had her reward when Burny flashed his black glasses at his friend and grinned. "She's got a good ear. Has she got a name?"

"I don't know. We didn't get that far."

"It's Laura," she said. "Plain Laura Brown."

"Pretty?" Burny asked his friend.

"She'll pass," he said flatly.

"And you're Burny," Laura said quickly. "But that's as far as I can go."

"Burny Malott," the guitarist told her. "And this character with the bark is Gil Bricker." There was affection in his voice and then a note of sulkiness as he added, "If you like jazz, you ought to hear Gil here play the piano. He's a good man. I ask myself how I'd get along without him."

"Cut that, will you?" Gil Bricker said. "What worries me is money. If we don't line up a date around this lake, we're going to be scratching for berries."

Burny frowned behind his black glasses, then shrugged. There was a sudden constraint between the two men. The guitar gave forth another dull chord as Burny said, "You don't need me. Line up a date for yourself."

"That'll be the day."

Laura watched Gil Bricker grab the coffeepot from the camp stove, slosh a mugful, and dump in sugar. But he was gentle as he bent down, fastened his friend's fingers around the cup, and said, on a laugh, "Drink up, genius. We've been together since West Berlin. If you can starve, who wants to eat?"

When he offered a cup to Laura, their eyes met, and she felt the pull of a smile. He was a nice person who could think of someone else—a man who could be tough and tender all at once. But it can't happen this fast, she thought as the half-sweet pang shot through her again and trembled off in a warning. Perhaps his concern for Burny was what touched her, she told herself.

She recalled how she had felt about Jenny before she had disappeared. A strong person had to accept responsibilities for the weaker. The trouble was, one could fail, and then guilt appeared.

As the three of them sipped coffee and the night bound them closer they relaxed into a give-and-take punctuated by the surface laughs of people newly met. At least she and Burny seemed to get along. Gil Bricker nursed his mug of coffee through stretches of uncooperative silence, which she found difficult to understand. Burny's remarks were accompanied by snatches of music now much lighter in tone, so wasn't Gil pleased? Perplexed, she watched him stand up suddenly and move with annoyance toward a canvas bag. He pulled an old shirt from it, came back, and tossed it over her bare shoulders.

"I thought you might be getting chilly," he said.

She wasn't. It was an extremely warm evening,

with a growing mugginess on the lake breeze that suggested storm, but now she understood.

She shrugged herself rather unhappily into the shirt, pulled her long hair free, and rolled up the cuffs. It must have belonged to the lanky guitarist, because the shirttails covered her knees.

And then she heard herself say, "I've got an idea! I know the manager at Lee's Landing, and I'll bet he could use you two in the Tavern Room. The resorters would be crazy about you, Burny. I know it."

"How about that?" exclaimed Gil, jumping in fast to back her up.

But Burny was wilting again. "Well, I don't know—" he said, plunking a tired chord.

"Please," she said. "I'm working a completely selfish angle, Burny. I've been trying to talk Mr. Samuels into letting me organize some swimming classes up there. If I could produce an attraction like you for his guests, he might listen to *my* deal."

Since she was already teaching swimming at Lee's Landing, she didn't know how long that improvised tale would hold up. But she hoped its appeal would reach Burny now.

His black glasses shone blankly in the lamplight. Gil flashed her a look of perplexity, then shrugged.

So she said bluntly, "After all, Burny, you do owe me something." And she won.

"O.K., chick," he said, with a dull flicker of music. "Gil can look him up sometime."

"Tomorrow," she announced, getting to her feet. "I'll pick you both up around noon."

Gil Bricker lifted his cup to her in silent acknowledgment, backing the gesture with the first smile she had earned from him. A smile too potent, too brief. And she wanted more than his own gratitude for helping Burny. Much more, she realized in confusion as she felt herself tremble.

"I can find my own way back," she said abruptly. "Don't bother."

"What's to bother?" Gil said, picking up a flashlight. "I always escort good fairies home."

She knew he meant to the broken-down pier, where she had tied up her outboard. But she wanted to be alone, to think undisturbed by his nearness. It was just possible that the situation had got out of hand already.

Whatever Gil's faults—and she told herself he probably had plenty of them, including a bullheaded loyalty—he'd never let anyone hurt this pitifully dependent friend of his. She'd probably despise him if he did.

The whole situation made her wonder about that mysterious girl Gil had mentioned, the one he had at first thought Laura was. She couldn't recall his tone when he spoke of her, but she seemed to feel it had been both bitter and revengeful.

Could that girl have caused trouble between the two musicians? If so, Laura decided heavily, that must have been the unforgivable sin . . .

Oppressively warm but with a breeze raking the

woods and a sprinkling of stars piercing the veil of cloud, night and darkness had finally covered Talisman Lake.

It would have been folly to take to the woods on foot again, so Laura followed Gil Bricker down through the reeds to the rowboat.

"Take it easy, kid," he had called back to his blind friend. "I'll just take her as far as her own boat."

Gil fastened the oars in place, then pulled out of the cove and up around the stone-beaked cliff and along the dark mass of the island.

Gil said, "If I owned a spot like this, I'd do something with it."

"For instance?"

"Put up some cabins. A lodge, maybe. Develop it."

"I thought you were a piano player."

"A living. I never had the spark like Burny, or even wanted it. That's what kills me—seeing him without the old genius."

The lake was choppy, and, caught on a breeze, the scent of wild honeysuckle reached them. As Laura let her fingers drag through the water, she was filled with the memory of another such night, years ago, when she had swum out here—alone in the promise of a storm, exulting in the risk.

That night she had been driven by the stirrings of adolescence and her heart had sung. Tonight, the stirring within her was sharper, heavier, carrying the ache of maturity.

"Keep close to shore so I can find the pier," she said, directing the flashlight beam.

But she didn't really want to reach any destination, to part from the silent man who was rowing with such precision and power, silent in the grip of his own thoughts. The choppy water and the rhythmic oars and the wind's strange blend of perfume and storm caught her up into an instant of torment the way Burny's music had. She raised both arms and lifted her hair from her neck, exulting as the air reached her damp flesh. Her smothered laugh made no sound; yet she felt sad, and a bit frightened by her feeling for this man who was a stranger.

"Isn't that the pier?" Gil asked, his voice again carrying that undertone of curtness.

"We've passed it," she said weakly, then stiffly, "Right oar. *Right.*"

When he reached out a hand to help her onto the rickety pier, she realized with a shock that she was considering deliberately stumbling against him.

"Thanks, Laura," he said. "You seemed to be just what Burny needed tonight."

"You think I'm uncomplicated enough?"

"I think we both owe you a lot already," Gil said.

"Well, you were right about him. Burny's sweet. I'd like to help pull him out of his troubles if I can. The mental ones, anyway."

She knew she ought to go, yet she stayed, rooted

24

to the unsteady pier. If she spoke, he'd have to stay awhile.

She blurted out, "How was he hurt, Gil? You said an—accident."

She had to wait. Gil's voice was hard, but what surprised her was that, once he'd started to explain, he seemed to want her to know.

"We were playing a night-club date in Chicago," he said. "One rainy night two hoodlums caught up with Burny in the alley. They only gave him a routine working over. Just brass knuckles and a gun butt. But they didn't know their own strength, and *I* was the one they'd been sent to get."

"Oh Gil—Gil, how awful. But why? I—I mean—"

"The police decided it was an ordinary mugging. Just one of those senseless things that make you boil. But by that time Burny was in the hospital with three doctors trying to save his eyesight. I didn't tell him the truth—that he'd taken a beating for me. I didn't see how knowing it would have helped him."

"It might have helped you," Laura said. "But I still don't understand. Why should that have left Burny so defeated? Not wanting to see?"

"A girl. What else?" Gil said. "She cut out on him when he needed her the most. She never came near the hospital. She cleared out of town and never even sent him a postcard with the time of day. She'd been working in the office at the club, and then later she'd moved into a specialty number. Lord! Sometimes when she'd step into the spotlight, you couldn't hear a glass clink in the whole place. But she had no real talent. Nothing but looks and nerve. Only, poor Burny had to fall in love with her."

"And you didn't?" Laura whispered.

"Off and on—I couldn't stay away from her. And she had this wealthy character named Warrigal on the string, besides. He was supposed to have been a gambler before he turned Big Business and made millions in real estate. Personally, I never saw him. He used to send around a limousine as big as a diesel for her. Then one night he sent me the message. Very polite too. Just, please stay away from his fiancée. That was the first I knew she was marrying anyone. Anyway, I *had* been staying away from her, but she must have given Warrigal the wrong impression. Two nights later, Burny was beaten up. I couldn't have proved it was meant for me, or why. And I couldn't tell Burny the truth. The poor guy had been walking around in a pink dream over her."

Laura said, "I suppose that's the girl you're looking for around here."

Gil nodded. "That's the one. She talked about this place once. She said she'd been born and raised around here. She didn't seem to have much use for it, but I figured if this was home, she might just come back here if she happened to be in trouble."

"Is she?"

"According to the grapevine, she is."

"What kind of trouble?" Laura asked through drying lips.

"I couldn't find out exactly. Somebody had seen her in Miami and said she looked scared to the bone. Maybe she'd broken up with Warrigal. Anyway, I wanted to find her, talk to her, bribe her to come back to Burny if I had to. I was going to *make* her come back to him for a while. The medics say a psychological lift may be all he needs to see again. Or a shock of some kind. Only now"—and Gil's voice quieted—"only now it doesn't seem like such a good idea after all."

Laura watched him turn away from her and fumble at the mooring line. The lifting wind picked up bits of angry water. It chopped at the boats and made the old pier groan, pulling the line so taut he was having trouble getting the boat untied.

Laura wondered why he had told her so much. Was it because this girl no longer mattered to him personally, or because he was trying to exorcise a memory that wouldn't rest? He wasn't the kind of man who could suffer guilt easily.

And the girl herself— *The beautiful girl from Talisman Lake!*

"What's her name?" Laura asked him, her voice muffled as the wind whipped her hair across her mouth.

"Talis. Jan Talis. Ever hear of her around here?

"No."

And Jenny's name is plain Jenny Brown, Laura thought. She closed her eyes for an instant, an aching tightness in her chest. So she was being silly. Premonitions happened all the time and came to nothing. Plenty of girls had been born and raised around Talisman Lake, and Jenny wasn't the only beautiful one.

Laura waited, but no relief came. She moved past Gil in such distraction that he shot her a look of uncertainty, then stopped working on the line and caught her arm.

"Laura? Laura, wait a minute. I didn't think this'd upset you. Why should it? It's no concern of yours."

"I'm glad."

"What's the matter with you? You wanted to know about Burny, so I told you. I thought it'd make it simpler for all of us if you knew his background. If we can arrange that date at the Lodge tomorrow, it'll mean a lot. To me, too. I'm really grateful, Laura. I know I've acted like a sorehead ever since I met you, but—"

"Have you? I hadn't noticed."

"What is the matter with you?"

"Nothing. May I go now? There's going to be a storm and—"

Nothing about her manner could have offered him any provocation; yet he reached up with a slow tentativeness to push his hands through her blowing hair, holding her with sudden roughness while he kissed her lips.

"May I go *now?*"

"Why not?" he said after a pause. She pulled off Burny's shirt and pushed it into Gil's hand, then she stumbled away from him, grateful for the sanctuary of her tossing boat. Her hands felt dead on the wheel, but she was faintly surprised that his kiss had moved her so little.

With an intense movement she pulled the starter and gunned a blast of sound across the night, completely shutting him off from her. She saw him lift his hand, but she turned her face toward the empty lake and opened the throttle, putting a white and furious wake behind her.

Unlike the old Lee's Landing where both she and Jenny had grown up against a background of shabby cabins and the dance hall where the dark sister Laura had sometimes been pressured into singing along with the combos hired by their father for the Saturday night dances, this new Lee's Landing projected an atmosphere of exclusiveness and wealth. Laura didn't miss the past—too much of it had been insecure—but she sometimes had trouble adjusting to the changes of the present—this new Lodge, for instance, gleaming with lights, terraced with glass to the water's edge, where sleek craft bobbed at anchor in the starlight.

A hundred yards out, her boat raced on past the

fieldstone bungalows and flowered lawns that rimmed the entire north shore now. She had to sail almost to the point, where the woods closed in again, before she reached the seclusion of her own private dock and the stocky cabin hidden by the curve of the shoreline.

Gosh, I'm tired, she told herself. *I'm tired and I'm a fool. What in heaven's name have I let myself in for?* She had agreed to burden herself with the problems of a blind guitar player who didn't want to see and of his guilt-ridden friend. She had practically promised to find them a job. She had even let the piano player kiss her, and then had gone cold in his arms.

As she scrambled onto her own dock, the memory of that kiss undid her again, thrusting her back to that other shaky pier beneath her, the smell of wild honeysuckle on the wind and the warmth of Gil's mouth on her own. She had felt so little at the time, distracted by that premonition about Jenny, but now she stood locked in the heavy and languid grip of memory. It was minutes before she started to move slowly again toward shore.

And just then, as the first rain struck harshly across her lips, she heard it—the faint rhythm of a jazz guitar moving across a hollow beat. She even turned to stare back stupidly across the lake. But Spider Island was much too far away for the sound of Burny Malott's guitar to reach her here.

She seemed to recognize the music. It was an

old Eddie Lang recording from her own collection. But she couldn't have gone off that morning and left her hi-fi on; she distinctly remembered having dusted the silent machine before she left. Besides, that particular record hadn't been on the turntable for days.

Just as the rain increased, her heart seemed to close like a fist. The cabin was dark, but she found the front door locked. It shouldn't be. It never was. She had to stop and remember where she had hidden a key. She let herself in just as the Eddie Lang recording ended.

The silence was harsh. It was broken by a click, followed by the almost soundless burr of the sapphire needle. Then she heard old Satchmo's trumpet.

One inadequate lamp burned orange beneath a dark shade, throwing shadows behind the divan and across the record files and up the knotty-pine walls. The cotton drapes were tightly drawn, making the room impossibly warm and sticky on such a night, and across one window—the window that faced in the direction of Lee's Landing—an Indian blanket had even been hung!

Laura snapped on another lamp, then leaned back against the door, shutting it with force, glad it was there to support her.

She had only a moment to wait. In the doorway from the kitchen appeared her sister's figure.

Chapter Three

"Hi, Laura. You scared the wits out of me."

It was Jenny, of the golden hair and the slim hazel eyes and the incredible beauty, the eternally unsatisfied Jenny whose face seemed shockingly thinner after three years and oddly drained of color, whose stare shot out one bright gleam of fear before the red lips achieved a smile and the hand holding a coffee cup gestured a greeting—a hand trembling so hard, its bracelets shook.

"Well, am I that bad a penny?" Jenny finally had to plead. "Can't you show even a little welcome?"

"Jenny—oh, honey—" Laura groaned. And they came together in the center of the room and clung, laughing so that they wouldn't cry. Jenny's arms tightened around Laura with an odd convulsiveness, the way they sometimes had when this younger sister was a child, needing comfort or help.

"It's all right," Laura heard herself murmur. "It's all right, honey."

"What is?"

"Well, I don't know. I just thought—"

"Let's don't think, shall we? I just want to look at you." And Jenny held her off. "Honestly, Sis, I'd forgotten anybody could look like you. It ought to be illegal."

"I was thinking the same thing about you," Laura sighed. "Too bad it never makes things easier for us."

"Oh, that. Men!" And Jenny turned away with a prowling nervousness to put her cup on a table. "At least your looks might do you some good if you'd clear out of this backwoods. Laura, how do you stand it?"

"No spirit and no ambition. Just a square, remember?"

"You sound proud of it."

"I'm not," Laura said quietly. "But it's just as easy to be satisfied with what you have."

"Is it? Anyway, for you it is. Everything neat and satisfying. Your housekeeping and your life."

"Did you come home just to quarrel with me?" Laura asked.

"I'm sorry," Jenny said, eyeing Laura with annoyed affection. "Sometimes I wish I were like you. Sometimes I even wish I could start all over and have it different."

"You could start now," Laura said uncertainly.

"Oh, bosh!" And Jenny's moment of wistfulness vanished. "I'm me. And you always make me feel like such a freak. Even after two minutes."

"I don't mean to. I'll get some more coffee."

Silent, Laura went past her into the kitchen and

rinsed Jenny's cup; then she let the water run cold across the throbbing pulse in her wrists.

Even in here the yellow-checked curtains had been drawn tight, suggesting that necessity to hide. Pulling them open, Laura tried to draw air into her lungs.

It was difficult to breathe, more difficult to think. She was not as habituated to Jenny's needling as she used to be.

Jenny loved her, she knew; yet Jenny seemed unable to give of that love without adding pain.

Moving abruptly, Laura unlocked the kitchen door and then stood by the screen, feeling the mist on her face as the downpour increased. She could see nothing beyond the cabin except the blackness of the crouching woods.

Always before, she had welcomed the isolation they gave her, but now, as if infected by the atmosphere that Jenny had brought with her, Laura shivered. And she had a strange feeling—as if someone or something were watching her through the pounding rain.

Laura stayed in the kitchen until she felt able to face her returned prodigal sister; then she came back into the main room of the cabin.

Jenny had switched off the lamp Laura had lighted, but the dim orange glow from the other lamp was sufficient to point up the bone-deep hollows beneath her beautiful cheekbones and the unnatural and distracted little movement of

34

clutching her silk robe around her as she dropped onto the divan—as if a chill had huddled her together. But the room was hot—stifling.

"Are you all right?" Laura asked.

"Why shouldn't I be?"

"Then let's have some air in here."

"Now wait a minute—" Jenny said sharply.

"Why? Don't be silly. No one can see in here," Laura said, removing the Indian blanket that Jenny had hung. "The woods are too thick between us and Lee's Landing—"

"But the lake—!"

"We're a hundred feet above the lake. What's the matter with you, anyway?" Laura asked, turning just in time to see a twist of fear cross Jenny's face like a spasm.

"I suppose you think I've lost my mind," the younger sister said, managing one of her appealing smiles.

"I think you're nervous and very tired, and I'm glad you're home. Beyond that, I don't know what to think, Jenny. About any of this."

"Well, I've been riding a bus all day. Then I had to walk all the way through the woods from the highway. I just wanted to relax. I wasn't sure about people looking in."

People! By comparison with the point, the moon was crowded. Watching her fair-haired sister reach for a cigarette, Laura again felt the quivering of a nervous bewilderment. Was she supposed to pry some explanations from her or simply chew her nails in patience?

Just then, as if mocking Laura's indecision, another recording dropped onto the turntable of the hi-fi. Another recording of the legendary Eddie Lang, which Jenny must have chosen. There were few all-time-great guitarists, and Lang had been on top.

How odd that Jenny should be partial to a guitar. How odd, Laura thought stiffly, that her own mind kept shying away from a coincidence that wasn't any coincidence at all. No more than Jenny's being here was a coincidence.

"You've built up quite a collection," Jenny said, eyeing Laura with that blend of hostility and affection. "Is this your only vice?"

"I don't know. I haven't counted them lately."

"Do you still sing, or was that a passing phase of our glamorous childhood?"

"Oh, I put on a stack of records sometimes and pretended I've got a voice. It helps pass an evening."

"I'll bet!" Jenny said, her slim eyes moving restlessly about the rather austere cabin. "Laura, how do you live like this? Nothing exciting but a pair of swim fins and a record player!"

"If you feel like that, Jenny, why did you come home?"

"I suppose because it is home," she answered dully. "Or used to be."

"But three years—" and Laura moved tensely,

unable to hold back the demand any longer. "Where have you been all this time?"

"Around. Chicago. Down to Florida for a while."

"Doing what?"

"Oh, things." Jenny shrugged, her remote carrying a trace of bitterness. "I had a good job modeling for a while. Fifty dollars a day, no less. I did some work on television. I even did the night-club circuits. But you know how it is—some man always comes along to ruin things."

"And you couldn't have written?"

"I wanted to. I almost did a couple of times." Jenny's eyes went cold. "But you never approved of the things I did when we were growing up, and I didn't want to be lectured long distance."

"But I'm still your sister, and I've missed you," Laura said with intensity. "Vanishing like that! I was half-sick with worry for weeks, Jenny. Didn't you even stop to think—"

"I never stop to think about anything. You ought to know that. And stop calling me Jenny. I'm not used to it any more. Jenny Brown! It sounds like a milkmaid. How far could I have gotten with a name like that? Or *did* I get anywhere? Anyway, I changed it to Jan. Jan Talis. I made up that last part from Talisman Lake."

Jenny giggled on a hollow note, dropped back onto the divan, and covered her eyes with one golden arm, the bracelets jangling, her cigarette spilling ashes.

The guitar music broke off, but nothing followed. Laura moved woodenly to the cabinet and flicked a switch. Now only the roar of the rain intruded.

Shivering slightly, Laura stared at the girl she had practically raised. This unkempt, frightened girl who was her own sister. Even Jenny's nails were carelessly chipped, one of them bitten down to the quick, Laura noticed—a telltale flaw that only deepened the cold ache around her heart. That familiar ache of love and annoyance and responsibility, wrenched by a new pity but only barely stirred by surprise.

So Jenny was Jan Talis, the girl Gil Bricker wanted to find. The girl responsible for Burny's condition—or at least callously implicated in it. The girl who had apparently left Gil simmering in a private torment of guilt.

She realized that Jenny's eyes—*Jan's* eyes—were fastened on her with a childlike intensity and that she was saying, "I'll be honest with you, Laura. I've been sick. I'm in a little trouble, too—not with the police or anything like that—just private trouble. I was hoping I could just stay here awhile and rest. Can I?"

"You know you can."

"I won't cause you any trouble or extra work. Honestly. I'll keep to myself. I'll help with the cooking. Remember the tuna things I used to make?" She was trying to joke, and she was running dangerously near hysteria. "I'll even dust in corners and keep my own room straight!"

"Honey, don't be silly—"

"But I don't want to see anyone."

"Well, all right—"

"I mean, I don't want anyone to know I'm here!"

"Why not?" Laura asked her steadily.

"Because I don't! Do you still have to snoop into my business?"

But then Jenny wrung her hands, clenching them between her knees as she sat up. Her face was white and miserable.

"Laura, I'm sorry," she whispered. "I've been a problem from way back. I wish I could be like you want me to. If things work out, I'll try. I promise! And I never did deserve you. Only please, *please* let me stay here without any more questions. And promise me—promise me—you'll keep quiet about it."

Chapter Four

Sometime during the night, the rain stopped.

But the dripping silence was worse. Again and again Laura punched wearily at her pillow, unable to quell the gnawing of her thoughts.

Why wasn't I firmer? Why didn't I make her tell me what kind of trouble she was in?

The answer was easy: *Because I don't want to know!* Because it was bound to involve Gil and Burny, tied up as they were in her sister's past. Even now, the moment Gil's dark image appeared on the jumbled screen of her bewilderment, she could feel a short circuit.

That kiss before the storm. If only Gil hadn't touched her. He had destroyed some inner nerve of her will. She had even felt unable to cope with her sister's rising hysteria and had agreed to keep Jan's presence in the cabin a secret for a while. From everyone.

Jan. Jan Talis. Already Laura seemed unable to think of her as "Jenny" any more. That once-familiar name seemed dead, a bit of their childhood buried beneath the weight of her own failings. But surely tomorrow things would fall into a better perspective, Laura told herself.

And the rain stopped, and she must have slept.

The morning was a jewel on the finger of late summer, polished to a perfection of sun and water that had already dotted Talisman Lake with hopeful fishermen.

It was such a sane day, Laura wanted to get out of the cabin before her sister awakened, before the plaguing sense of responsibility and helplessness set in again. Moving as quietly as possible, she forced herself to eat an adequate breakfast.

With three solid hours of swimming classes ahead of her before noon, she could at least stoke up on vitamins if not on peace of mind. At last, clutching her clipboard with the day's swim schedules, plus a beach towel and a bag containing a change of clothing so that she needn't return until evening, she was able to slip from the still-silent cabin and hurry down the reeded path to the dock.

What a heavenly morning as she spun her trim red outboard into deep water. She was still edgy with fatigue—she told herself she'd have to watch any tendency toward snappishness with her timid moppets—but once she had reached Lee's Landing and the morning's routine was under way, once the splashing and the silliness and the correcting had begun, she felt herself regain a welcome normalcy.

When her tadpole classes in shallow water were over, it felt good to stretch out with the advanced youngsters for the long swim to the raft.

Pulling herself onto it, she ordered, "All right,

now. Line up, but wait for my signal. Free form for fifty yards, then back. And remember—kick from the hips and no sloppy elbows. Ready? Go!"

They hit the water with the precision of dolphins and lit out straight in the direction of Spider Island.

Laura drew a hard breath and stared across the shining water, wondering suddenly if either Gil or Burny might not be doing the same thing. She had promised to talk to Mr. Samuels about them, and she hadn't. She had promised to pick them up at noon, and the sun was already directly overhead.

Balanced for an instant on the swaying raft, feeling the heat and beauty of the day, she felt a flash of power. *I won't go near them,* she told herself. *I won't do anything. It's simple.*

And, of course, it was impossible. The moment of freedom passed, and she was involved again. One did this and that because one had promised to. But perhaps her promise needn't commit her to anything more than trying to carry it out.

It was well past noon before she could change into a red-flowered skirt and black thonged sandals in one of the lakeside cabanas and then hurry along the gravel paths to the office of the manager.

The chromium fittings matched Mr. Samuels' thin gray hair, and whenever he smiled at her, she felt she ought to curtsy. He was as neat as an IBM machine and just as business-like, and if he ever could have seen the garish resorters her father had ruled over on this very spot, he would have been visibly shaken. People like that should remain at the other end of the lake, he had long ago decided.

However, he had always treated her with a friendly deference, Laura had noticed. Perhaps because he considered her a relic left over from the dark ages.

Now, listening to her, Mr. Samuels finally said with a hint of distaste, "A guitar player? Probably with sideburns and a wiggle. Frankly, Laura, I can't see our guests enjoying that kind of entertainment."

"But Burny Malott is nothing like that. He's unique, Mr. Samuels. He's a genius, really. He could play on a concert stage and have people enchanted."

"But he's blind, you say."

"Well, not exactly. It's what the doctors call psychological blindness. He had an accident, but he'll see again as soon as he wants to see. I know that sounds odd, but it's the reason why it's so important for him to get back to work again."

"Jazz musicians are difficult enough to handle," Mr. Samuels said. "I don't like the idea of hiring one that's psychologically unstable as well."

"But he isn't, Mr. Samuels. I mean, there's nothing odd or beat about him. He's just a rather sad young man with a marvelous talent. Please—won't you at least listen to him?"

Mr. Samuels put his fingertips together. It was a bad sign. He said, "You seem rather concerned about this, Laura. How long have you known these two men?"

"Only since yesterday," she had to admit. "I found them camped out on the island. But I've heard Burny play, Mr. Samuels. Like—well, like nobody but himself! That was enough for me."

"Hm. I see," the manager said disapprovingly. "What about the piano player? Does he have a problem, too?"

"Gil Bricker? Just money, I guess," she said, a bit too lightly. "As a matter of fact, he looks more like an athlete than a musician."

"You mean solid. Well, that's something. Very well. But I'm promising nothing. Absolutely nothing, Laura. If you can have them back here in an hour, I'll try to audition them."

"Even sooner! And thank you so much, Mr. Samuels. I know you won't regret it."

But by the time Laura returned with Gil and Burny in tow, she was half regretting it herself.

They had been waiting for her in their rowboat by the rotting pier, and Gil had snapped, "What kept you?" But as he had helped Burny find his footing in the outboard, there had been a smile for her and a little nod of gratitude—though nothing more. The ride back had been as unsatisfying as it had been fast.

Laura had felt depressed and nervous, and the image of the sister she couldn't talk about had clouded her silences. Gil had behaved like some tourist with only the scenery on his mind, while

Burny, slumped in the back seat, had nursed his guitar as if he expected to drown with it.

Now, crossing the lobby of the Lodge toward the Tavern Room, Laura was conscious that they both needed haircuts and that they might, at least, have tucked their clean-enough shirts into their unpressed slacks.

Beatniks? What else! She felt herself flush.

She realized that curious glances were following them, and she wished that Mr. Samuels didn't have to see them at all and waste his time.

Since the Tavern Room at Lee's Landing didn't open until the correct cocktail hour of four P.M. it was empty when Laura, trailed by her two unkempt muscians, pushed open the driftwood door. But not completely empty, she realized as the door sighed shut. A busboy was polishing glasses in the underwater glow of the bar, and two cleaning women were gossiping in the corner.

Gil came to a shuffling halt, the hand of his blind friend still gripping his arm for guidance.

"What's the word, man?" Burny inquired, shifting his guitar and turning his black glasses here and there like a bony owl.

"Intimate as a kiss," Gil told him. "You'll fracture 'em in here, Burny. I can hardly wait."

Laura's eyes had adjusted enough for her to realize that Mr. Samuels was already ensconced in one of the booths, his chromium ballpoint poised over a sheaf of papers, like a judge about to initial the execution decree.

One hour, the manager of the resort had stipulated. Theye weren't late, but Mr. Samuels certainly stiffened when she made the introductions.

Nodding, he said briefly, "Any time you're ready," and went back to his padded enclosure.

Laura tried to smile encouragingly at Gil, but his face had hardened and she could sense his sudden discomfort.

Laura watched Gil pull up a bar stool for his slump-shouldered pal, then give the small piano a push and a glide until it came to rest where it suited him.

They were a pair, all right. Burny looked like an underfed scarecrow with a shag of red hair, and Gil might have been a wrestler—big shoulders, big hands, and a worried face.

Searching for Laura suddenly, he even gave her one of his dark smiles. She felt her lips move in uncertain reply, but then she realized he wasn't even seeing her. He was attuned to Burny like a gunner to his sergeant.

He doesn't even care about playing, she realized then. *It's a business with him. What grips him so hard is that guilt about Burny.*

"What'll it be?" Burny asked with a discouraged chord.

"You name it. I'll ride along."

So Burny half bent his head as if to listen to his inner demon, shrugged, then let his thin fingers pick out a little music. The blue notes flickered, and the beat mounted. Then Gil's piano came weaving in as dark and easy as a nighttime breeze. It was fire and ice cream. Voodoo and pain and a long-lost mile from nowhere.

They played oldies, and they improvised on a Cuban beat. They played hill-billy music with the tonalities of Bach, and then they played simple jazz. Well, not simple. But it didn't matter what they played.

The cleaning women stood still with their mops, and the busboy was now polishing the bartop with quiet elbows. Even Mr. Samuels had laid aside his pen and put his fingertips together.

Somehow Laura found herself leaning against the tiny piano, and somehow she found herself humming along with them in an unconscious intimacy of mood, lost and happy, putting in the words when she knew the words, the way she did lonely evenings at the cabin, listening to her recordings, joining in with the jazz greats she treasured, singing along without half knowing it.

She must have followed them all the way through "Blue Moon" and "Temptation" and "Summertime." And when the music stopped, something was very wrong with the silence.

No one moved. Gil's stare was almost angry in its intensity, while Burny's blind face made Laura think of a boy coming face to face with a lollipop tree all shining and full of goodies.

47

The guitar player said softly, "Wow! Did you hear what I heard?"

"You mean perfect pitch? But the tone didn't project. It was immature," Gil said.

"Immature!" Burny breathed. "Immature as a lost angel on a street corner. And that timing! Nobody can learn it. You're either born with it or else."

Laura's embarrassment was putting her through an ugly moment. How could she have let herself go like that, perhaps ruining the whole audition for them? She felt all hands and hot face, with nowhere to hide.

"I'm terribly sorry—" she began thickly.

And Burny said, "Do that again, will you?"

"What?" Laura asked.

"That beat, chick, that beat."

"You mean sing? Look. Honestly. I feel terrible. I didn't even realize—"

"We know you didn't," Gil said, "so just do what he asks, will you? We can all cry over it later."

So she tried to get through *Sweet and Lovely* with Gil nodding impatiently whenever she fluffed the lyrics and with her voice finally cracking, fading, dropping her into an angry and embarrassed silence. The joke—if it was a joke—was no longer just funny.

"Did you ever sing before?" Gil wanted to know.

"No. Not really. I mean, a little, maybe; but it was nothing."

"Very clear. Let's try it again. Did you ever sing before?" Gil repeated curtly.

"No! Well, kid stuff at the local dances ages ago. But nobody thought I could sing. I was an ornament."

"Will you just be quiet a minute?" Burny said, his voice catching on its own excitement as he came fumbling along the piano in search of her, his guitar banging clumsily as he gripped her hand. "Listen, chick," he said, "let's just say you've got a quality in your voice. A kind of innocent beat. You don't know how to use it right, but it's there. And it's one-in-a-million stuff. It's what makes singers like Peggy Lee and Ella Fitzgerald and—"

"Thanks. Can I go now?" Laura said stiffly.

"What's the matter with you?" Gil said. "The guy's telling you you've got a future. Not leprosy."

"You're darned right," Burny said with animation. "It'd mean hard work—the old Simon Legree bit—but in a year, who knows? A million-hit record for us, maybe. This business can win you a jackpot or a dime."

"Or a headache," Gil said, rippling off a flat arpeggio.

"But I don't want a future," Laura said with difficulty. "I like it the way I am. Here. Doing what I like to do."

"Teaching kids the old dog paddle," the blind

guitarist said impatiently. "That's an excuse, not a career."

"I don't *want* a career! Maybe this isn't a joke after all, but it's pretty ridiculous. I have a job I like, and I'm not the least bit ambitious. My summers at Talisman lake suit me fine."

"What do you do with the winters?" Burny asked.

"I teach physical therapy at the county center in Lakeville."

"Will you dig that?" Burny groaned. "What does this girl look like, anyway? She sounds like my Aunt Fanny with the muscles."

Gil said drily, "She could stand in a spotlight, and nobody would care if she opened her mouth. But she doesn't want to sing, so let's stop selling."

"Thank you. I don't!" she said. "It's out of the question."

Coming up from behind them, Mr. Samuels said pleasantly, "Then perhaps we can get down to business, gentlemen. If you'd care to talk salary in my office."

"You mean we're hired?" Gil asked.

"Until the end of the season. Eight till midnight every night. Starting tonight, if that's agreeable."

"How about that?" Gil grinned and then came off his piano bench to reach for Mr. Samuels' authorizing handshake.

But Burny hadn't moved. It hurt Laura to look at his face, because she sensed how hard he was straining to see her, to reach her. When Gil

touched his arm—the signal to lead him away—
Burny shook him off with a sudden irritability, as
if his own weakness shamed him.

"Come on. The man wants to sign us up," Gil
said, a frown of uncertainty in his dark eyes.

"O.K. Fine. But come back and talk to her, will
you? Convince her? She doesn't seem to realize
what I can do with that voice. *Make* her want to
work with us."

Chapter Five

But Laura wasn't waiting to hear what anyone could do with her voice.

The unexpected twist to the audition in the Tavern Room had both embarrassed and upset her. Burny was certainly in deadly earnest about what he probably considered his "discovery," but her own reaction had been anything but pleased.

The possibility of letting herself be turned into a professional singer left her cold. What was wrong with remaining a nobody, loving the place where you'd been born and wanting to remain part of it? she wondered irritably. What good had it done Jan to run away from her own background —for the glitter and the trouble and the fear and the failures?

And besides all that, Laura wanted to be free of them—Gil and Burny. She was too involved already, involved on levels of perplexity and complication that frightened her.

Anxious to get away from the Lodge before either Gil or Burny left Mr. Samuels' office, Laura hurried back down to the row of bright-striped cabanas on the lake front. She had to change back into a bathing suit, and haste made her clumsy. Grabbing clipboard and beach bag, she set off for the pier on a quick trot, securing her long black hair with a clip as she went.

This trip across the lake to the south shore had better be fast. She was unforgivably late for her first private lesson of the afternoon, and Gil Bricker was going to make her later.

She knew it the instant she saw him striding down from the Lodge to head her off at the pier.

"Laura—!"

"I'm sorry," she said, "but I was due across the lake twenty minutes ago."

"But just a minute, can't you?"

"I don't think so."

She tossed her things onto the red-padded seat of her outboard, drew a hard breath, and turned to face him, a bit surprised to find that same trace of suspicion in his stare that had marked their first moments of meeting on the island.

This pier was wide, broad-planked, and safe. They stood in sunlight, with the waves shimmering across the water. But an impression of being alone with him on a strip of insecurity gave her voice its note of faintness.

She said, "I know what you're going to ask me, but the answer is no."

"Can you tell me why not?"

"Because I have an overdeveloped sense of responsibility, Gil. It seldom seems to help anyone, and it often hurts me."

"I don't see how it could hurt you to humor Burny for a little while."

"I haven't the time."

"It wouldn't take much of your time. We could work it in any way to suit you. A session here, a session there."

Gil paused, and when she stooped to free her mooring line, he reached down irritably and jerked it taut again.

"Look, Laura. I don't blame you for not warming up to Burny's idea. You may have the talent, but becoming a professional is a rough job. It isn't worth the grief unless you're made for it. I don't think you are, myself. But you saw the way it hit him back there—like a kid begging for Christmas. For the first time in months he *wanted* something. I haven't seen him like that since he took that beating for me and wound up blind."

"I'm sorry about that. But Burny's your responsibility if you want to think so. Not mine."

"You didn't talk like that out on the island. You even saved his life."

"I'd have done the same for anyone."

"But you said you'd like to help straighten him out. Any way you could."

"I did. And I've tried to help! I took you to Mr. Samuels, didn't I?"

"You did. You even lied a little to get Burny to come."

"Lied?"

"Twisted the truth, then—is that better? You're

54

already teaching swimming here. Samuels told us you were the best instructor he's ever had."

"Oh, that. I just wanted to put a little pressure on Burny. I thought it might help to—" She bit her lip.

"See what I mean? Yesterday you were all on Burny's side. Today you've flipped. I don't get it."

"At least you got the jobs."

"At a nice figure," Gil admitted. "And I'm grateful." His gaze seemed both sharp and critical. "We also got some information. It seems your father once owned this whole shore. It also seems we've been squatting on your island."

"So?" she muttered, stooping to untie the line he'd pulled tight.

"So why hide it?"

"Hide it!" Her head flew back. "Listen. I didn't tell you because I didn't want you trying to pay me any rent."

"Which we intend to do."

"Don't be ridiculous!"

"You avoided mentioning one other little item," Gil said. "Samuels called you a 'native.' "

"Born and raised in these parts."

"That wasn't important, either."

"It might be if you happened to know this Jan Talis I wanted to find," Gil said, a muscle working in his cheek.

"And I told you I've never even heard of such a person!" Armed with a half-truth, she could at least meet his eyes.

"Ever since I mentioned her, something's had you upset," Gil said. "You froze up on a kiss, and now you're freezing up on Burny. I ask myself why. No answer. Then I look at you again, and I get unhappy."

"Because I bother you!"

"Because you're too beautiful," Gil said. "I see a face like yours, and I wonder what's going on behind it. Ever since Jan, I find myself making comparisons. It's illogical, but I do it anyway. And in your case, I'm sorry. I almost wish we could go back out to your island and start over again."

"Poor timing and the wrong people," she said lightly as their glances held.

His own broad cheekbones wore a flush. She watched him rip the line free and drop it into her hand. She felt the tug of her outboard as it rode the swells.

Gil pulled himself back from a moment of staring down into the water. "Samuels offered to put us up at the Lodge, but I'd rather rough it, and Burny says the island's O.K. with him. Is it all right if we stay put?"

"Of course."

"Rent?" he asked with a brief grin.

"Now, listen—"

"Then I'll build you something. How about a new dock for the cove? I like to fool around with tools. It's a relief from those eighty-eight little keys."

"Do anything you like," she said. "But how are you going to get back and forth every night? Row?"

"Samuels is loaning us something faster. One of those little aluminum jobs, I guess."

"They're for the guests," she explained. "You can buy gas at Conover's Store on the west shore." And when she had the red wheel in her hand, she smiled back up at him. "I'm glad you're all set, Gil."

"Yeah. Dandy," he mumbled. His hands were deep in his pockets, and his white shirt flapped in the breeze. "Can you catch our opening tonight?" he asked her.

"I doubt it."

"I wish you would, Laura. For Burny's sake."

If he hadn't said that, she might have answered him. Spinning the wheel, she felt the lash of spray across her stiff lips. Everything for Burny. Gil made sounds like a cracked record repeating itself in an empty room.

Chips of brilliance danced off the water and cut her eyes. She wished it were evening and cooler and time to go home. But she remembered that she didn't even have a home now. She'd turned it into a hideout for the girl Gil couldn't get over.

The sunset finally came and with it a trace of the coolness Laura had longed for.

She had swum so hard all afternoon that even her legs and shoulders ached. And probably some

57

of her pupils now bore her a grudge. *I really worked them,* she thought wryly.

Steering her slim red craft along the west shore of the lake, she cut across the wake of a sailboat and headed in toward the cluster of white buildings at the end of a dirt road that curved back sharply into the woods. The post office and the gas station had modern fronts, but Conover's General Store had changed little since her childhood.

In those days, clutching pennies given her by some vacationer from her father's old resort, Laura had often hiked down through the woods just to stand in front of Ed Conover's candy case and savor the delight of making her own choice— licorice sticks or jawbreakers?—free from her younger sister's petulant demands for something else.

The candy case was gone now, and in its stead gleamed an open freezer, neon-lighted and displaying the fruits and vegetables of modern living. Laura passed on to a bin of fresh peas, locally grown. These she would buy for supper, she decided, with some fresh tomatoes and two thick steaks, which she couldn't really afford. But the prodigal was home again, and how could she welcome Jan on a can of beans?

"*Two* steaks, Laura?" Ed Conover inquired, holding his gleaming knife over the haunch of beef. He was still nonprogressive enough to butcher his meat to a customer's needs and to give advice to the young. "Sounds like a man for supper."

58

"Anyway, a guest." She smiled.

"Well, it oughta be a man," he said. "You live like a hermit off there at the point. Summer after summer ever since your dad died. Things ain't the same now—even a girl with your looks has got to go out after a husband. I been telling you that—"

"Everytime I come in," she laughed. "I'm working on it, too. You'll see."

"I'll bet," he grumbled.

She added a carton of cigarettes to her order for Jan and stacked up on magazines.

"Laura—?" Ed Conover came around the counter. "How about taking along a kitten, too?"

"Oh, *no!* Not again," she said with exasperation.

"Yup. The resorters bring their cats, and the cats have kittens. Happens every summer."

And in the winter the poor lost things turned wild, left to prowl the woods and kill off the rabbits and squirrels.

"Six of 'em this time. Siamese, I think. They're out under the tree in a chicken crate. Help yourself."

But she didn't want any strays. The number of orphan kittens born at Talisman Lake was astronomical, and she was tired of feeling indignant about it. Nor had she any intention of adopting one. Not even this skinny little thing with the turquoise eyes and the hungry squeak.

"Hey, you," she whispered. And when he was nestled against her cheek, he burst into a purr big enough to split himself wide open.

59

"Phut-Phat," she said. "That sounds Siamese-ish from somewhere."

He slit his blue eyes at her and grinned, and with a sigh of defeat she gently pushed the skinny orphan down into a corner of her grocery carton and lowered the lid.

Blind guitar players or long-lost sisters or abandoned kittens. Just let that sense of responsibility get to aching, and she was a pushover. No, a fool. But Jan would like the kitten, too, and Phut-Phat ought to keep her sister amused at the lonesome cabin.

Picking up her carton, Laura stepped from behind the tree into the road. She didn't look, and by then it was too late. The car took the curve in a cloud of dust, dug in with its power brakes, and managed to miss her by inches. By that time she had stumbled backward and was sitting flat on the ground, the carton of groceries still clutched in her arms.

The breath must have been knocked out of Phut-Phat too, because all was silent beneath the lid.

"You must not want to live," the driver of the car said, piling out to help her up and get her organized again.

"There's a curve there!" she exclaimed. "You didn't even slow down."

"I would have if you'd stepped out sooner."

"Thanks. But you were doing over sixty!"

"Seventy," he said.

The car was a pale gray Chrysler convertible, with gray leather upholstery to match, and a pair of strange looking dogs lolling on the back seat. They had cup-shaped ears, eyes that slanted into their sandy coats, and a look as primitive as jackals about them. They were chained to the car doors, Laura noticed thankfully. Otherwise slaughter might have ensued if the kitten so much as squeaked.

"Are you all right?" their master asked.

"I think so. Bruised but conscious."

His crew cut was thick and more blond than gray, his skin evenly browned, his jaw heavy. The platinum ring he wore on his left hand—a kind of signet ring with a dog's head on it—was so large, she wondered why it didn't overbalance him. He was dressed conservatively, otherwise—gray slacks, gray shirt, gray sports shoes.

The man in gray, she thought. *Even his eyes.* They were pale, too, and blanker than chalk dust.

But his smile was pleasantly direct. "Here. I'll take that," he said, and removed the grocery carton from her grasp. "The least I can do is give you a lift."

"I came by boat."

"That's unfortunate. The next time I'll have to run you down in the water."

Despite her protests, she had to let him return her to the red outboard. After he had deposited her carton, he turned to stare back along the shore.

61

"This can't be Lee's Landing," he said with a twisting lip.

"No. You took the wrong turn on the main highway. You'll have to go back, then north about five miles. There'll be a fancy gate. If you have a reservation and you're in *Who's Who*, they may let you in. But they'll worry."

"I don't anticipate any trouble," he said, smiling, as he eased his weight onto both feet. "I have about a week. I thought I'd get in a little hunting."

"Hunting? You mean fishing, don't you? There's plenty of game in the northern part of the state, but you'll find the pickings pretty slim around here."

"Then I may fish," he said mildly.

He wasn't as tall as either Gil or Burny, but he made Laura feel decidedly short. Short, sunburned, and home-grown.

He said, "My name is Harrison Lasher. I wish you'd look me up. I'd like to do something to make up for almost killing you."

"How nice. I may even let you," she lied, and nimbly jumped down into her boat.

Phut-Phat the kitten had managed to claw open the carton lid and was hung over the edge, complaining mewfully.

"Heh, you again!" she said softly, scooping him up. "You want to fall in and be a minnow's dinner?"

Behind her on the pier, the man named Harrison Lasher made some kind of movement, some kind of sound. Turning, she froze. His face was different, distorted—the mouth twitching, the eyes almost blazing.

"The filthy beast!" he said. "Throw it overboard!" But even as she stared, he recovered himself with an effort and then laughed. "I'm sorry," he said. "But the cat startled me, and I have rather a morbid dislike of cats. Some people do, you know. It even has a medical name—ailurophobia."

"This isn't a cat, it's a kitten," she said, still clutching the tiny thing against her racing heart.

"All the same—" and he was normal again, smiling down at her in the boat. "I just happen to prefer dogs," he said.

Prehistoric little monsters he has to keep on chains, Laura thought. His nonsense had bothered her so much, she could scarcely bid him a civil good-by.

Beneath the last flareup of the sunset, the lake was a glittering red, but by the time she reached the point, the water had faded to opalescence and the woods were shadowy.

Taking the reedy path, Laura approached her cabin with a feeling of reluctance. But she saw that at least Jan had got over the silliness about locking herself in and shrouding the windows. The room was undusted, unswept, and stale with the smell of cigarettes.

Laura stopped for an irritated moment to switch off the hi-fi—had it been going all day? she wondered—and then went into the kitchen and unloaded the groceries. She set Phut-Phat on the floor with a saucer of milk and a bit of the raw steak, and then turned to contemplate the sink, which held Jan's dirty lunch dishes.

"Jenny?" she called sharply. "I mean Jan?"

Laura hadn't meant to enter her sister's bedroom, but as she passed the door, impulse was too strong. The room was a mess. Bed still unmade. Dresser cluttered with powder, cigarette butts, and a trio of empty coke bottles. Jan hadn't even bothered to unpack her small traveling case. It lay open on a chair, spilling hose, costume jewelry, and a lace nightgown.

Despite the habit of years of automatically picking up after her sister, Laura meant only to straighten Jan's belongings so that the case could be closed. But something held the lid open. She pushed down twice, then removed a pair of black suede pumps. Underneath was a stack of green printed paper, bound by a thick rubber band.

Laura picked it up and then turned it over with a complete sense of unreality. Green paper bills. Green paper money. In fifties, in hundreds, in dozens of hundreds.

Lying so innocently upon her palm, there must have been at least four or five thousand dollars—in cold, unbelievable cash.

Chapter Six

From behind Laura at the bedroom door, her sister's flat and frightened voice demanded, "What are you doing in my things? Do you think you're still my nursemaid? How dare you come snooping in here?"

"Your room was so untidy," Laura whispered. "I only meant to straighten the case—I— don't understand, Jan—what *are* these?" Laura said, holding out the stack of bills.

"What do they look like?"

"Well, money. I—I know that. But so much—thousands of dollars."

Meeting Jan's slim eyes against the dreadfully thin and golden face, Laura had never felt more inadequate and yet responsible. She had practically raised this child—no child any longer, certainly! —and now she was allowing her to hide in her own cabin—like a criminal, a thief?

"Jenny, honey, nobody wants to snoop, but—"

"Then don't. Jenny's dead. There's only Jan Talis now and the stupid mistakes she's made."

"Is that why you're so afraid of someone? Because of this money?"

"The money! I don't even want it. I'd never touch a nickel of it," Jan said. "But I took it, if that's what you mean."

"*Took* it?" Laura whispered. "You mean you stole it?"

She watched the red lips quiver, then curl into a bleak smile.

"I took it because I had to!" Jan sobbed, and then suddenly, "*You!* The isolated beauty with the bleeding heart. What do you know about having to claw your way around? With hating the way things turn out. What right have you to condemn me for anything!"

"I'm not condemning you," Laura said. "I never have. I just wish I knew how to help—"

"Well, you don't, so let me alone. But the police aren't looking for me, if that's what's worrying you."

"Then who is?" Laura asked with quiet pain as she dropped the money back into Jan's traveling case.

"Nobody. I've been sick, I told you. I just want to stay here and rest. Is that asking too much? I can, too—if you'll just keep quiet about me and stop prying into what doesn't concern you."

The two sisters stared at each other across the cluttered bedroom. Caught in an angle of the mirror, Laura could see them both. Strangers to each other, sharing nothing but the difficult heritage of too much beauty and of being linked somewhere in the depths of childhood. Somehow that link of

66

love always held. It held tenaciously. While on the surface came that plea of Jan's: *Help me but let me alone!*

"I've always tried to," Laura even said aloud.

"What?"

"Nothing. It doesn't matter," Laura said with an empty gesture as she left the room.

And there was still dinner to get. The ordinary things that had to go on no matter what.

Stooping in the kitchen to light the broiler for the steaks, Laura reached out to caress the kitten, who squatted on a square of linoleum like some tiny idol—skinny tail drawn across feet no bigger than dimes. now that he'd eaten, he looked so wise and clever that she had to grin in spite of herself.

"Salaam, oh mighty one. But watch it. You don't own the place yet."

A quick shower and change while the steaks sizzled made the world seem less black. When Laura returned to the kitchen, Jan was there too, the kitten curled against her bare shoulder.

"Oh, Laura, he's a doll. Is he yours?"

"Ours, I guess, now that you're home," she said quietly as she reached for the salad bowl. "I picked him up at Conover's. Just another stray."

"Aren't we all," Jan said, rubbing her cheek against the tiny creature. "Has he got a name?"

"Phut-Phat. I think that's Siamese for 'beautiful.'"

"Criminy. Him, too? Oh, well—" And as Jan's silk-gold hair lay across the kitten's fur, Laura watched her face grow soft and young, an almost forgotten innocence shining through. Even her eyes betrayed a moment's happiness before they clouded over again and met her sister's gaze.

"Laura, I'm sorry," she said. "I don't know why I talk to you the way I do. You're the only person in the world who means a thing to me."

"You're always sorry and you always repent," Laura said with a weary jab at a tomato.

"And you always forgive me," Jan said.

"I suppose I do. But things are different this time. You're in some kind of an ugly mess—no, don't lie about it, Jan. You are. But you expect me to walk around like a wooden Indian—seeing nothing, hearing nothing, not even asking you any questions."

"Wooden monkey, dear, not Indian," Jan said. "I'm only asking you to keep quiet about my being here. It won't be for long. I hope."

"That's not so simple. I'm getting involved along with you. Whether I want to or not."

"That's ridiculous," Jan said, but now her gaze was narrowing again across the kitten's head.

"Is it?" Laura exclaimed and turned on her sister with intensity. "Then what am I supposed to do about a couple of men I found camped out on the island yesterday? One of them happens to be a blind guitar player named Burny Malott, and the other one's named Gil. Gil Bricker."

Jan's fingers must have tightened on the kitten, because Phut-Phat let out an angry squeak and

68

clawed her. Bending to put the Siamese back on the floor, Jan asked evenly, "What do you know about Gil Bricker?"

"I know he plays the piano. I also know he's looking for a girl named Jan Talis because of the way she treated his friend Burny. Awkward, isn't it? Especially when this Jan Talis turns out to be my own long-lost sister who expects me to hide her like a criminal and ask no questions!"

"I'm not a criminal," Jan said. "Just get that straight!"

"All right. I'm sorry," Laura whispered.

But as Jan continued to stand there, looking trapped and injured, Laura turned back in despair to finish tossing the salad. She forked the sizzling steaks from beneath the broiler, added a bit of butter and garlic salt, and poured two cups of steaming coffee. She sat down across from Jan's empty chair, and after a moment Jan slid in opposite her, a sulky and heart-breaking child. In spite of herself, Laura reached impulsively across the table, and for a moment their fingers clung.

"Look," Laura pleaded. "Just tell me this. Does that money belong to either Gil or Burny?"

"It belongs to nobody now." Then Jan surprised her with an after-hoot: "To those two jokers? They never had five dollars between them." Her eyes dropped to fasten moodily on her steak. She jabbed it with a fork, then shrugged. "I suppose I might as well tell you. Then maybe you'll stop pestering me. I met 'em both about a year ago in Chicago. We were working at the same night club. They made the music, and I did a sort of specialty number. Anyway, Burny Malott had to fall in love with me. I guess for real," Jan added with a half-regretful smile of remembrance.

"He was always so absorbed in his music, the thing must have hit him pretty hard. Well, for a while I was almost in love with him, too. I really was, Laura. But then Gil Bricker started to worry about my effect on Burny and his music. He'd always acted like he was Burny's guardian angel. Gil tried so hard to keep me away from Burny, he fell for me himself."

Again a faint shrug lifted Jan's shoulders, but now her face was cold.

"For a while I thought it was the real thing with Gil. You've seen him—you can imagine what it was like. Then he began to feel guilty and mixed up—having to lie to Burny about us. Then Gil decided to break up with me. I didn't care very much. By then I'd gotten sick of the pair of them, and besides, I'd met someone else. A man named Warrigal. Harry Warrigal. It was wonderful at first. I was crazy about him. I thought he was everything I'd ever prayed for, and he wanted me to marry him. He had so much money, I was dazzled. He owned a resort hotel in Las Vegas and another one in Florida, but he wouldn't talk to me about his business. He said a beautiful woman wasn't supposed to think unless a man told her to. If he couldn't buy what he wanted, he'd get it some other way. He liked to hurt and humiliate people —make them grovel. I didn't realize that at first."

Jan swallowed, and her lips twitched nervously.

"Harry had already told me to break off with Gil, but I said I couldn't. I didn't mean to lie about that. Gil had already broken up with me, but I just wanted to make Harry jealous. Harry had never been near the club himself. I didn't know what he meant. But he must have hired a couple of hoodlums to warn Gil off with a beating, and they got to Burny by mistake."

Jan leaned forward then, her fingers picking nervously at her ragged thumbnail, her voice beginning to shake.

"I felt awful when I heard about it, Laura. Honestly! I'd have gone to see Burny in the hospital, but Harry threatened me. Then he got nice again and said we were flying down to Florida. I could have anything I wanted for a wedding present, he promised. We'd be married in Miami. By then I just wanted to get away from him, but I couldn't. You don't know what a man like that is like! I was afraid of him. I knew by then he was crazy jealous, and I was beginning to think he might really be crazy! Psycho. I had my own private suite in his Miami hotel, but when I went out, Harry was always with me, and when I stayed in my rooms, I felt I was being constantly watched—by the maid or the bellboy or somebody. When I'd try to get an outside line, the switchboard somehow wouldn't put me through. I couldn't even mail a letter to Burny or phone him long distance."

Jan finished on a cry of angry distress, "I don't see why Gil can't forget the whole thing and leave me alone! I've got enough grief of my own!"

"So has Burny," Laura said as a feeling of illness spread through her. "He's not really blind, Jan—he just can't see. He doesn't want to see, I guess."

"Well, that figures. Burny had a habit of sulking behind Gil whenever he couldn't get what he wanted."

"He's not sulking now. He can't *see!*" Laura explained. "He needs a psychological lift. All Gil could think of was making you go back to him for a while."

The younger sister stared. "So Gil's trying to work off his guilt on me. Or do you suppose he wants me back himself and won't admit it?"

"I have no idea," Laura said too loudly, and in the moment of silence that followed, she had to sit still beneath a sudden gleam from the knowing eyes that watched her.

"I doubt that," Jan purred. "You seem to know quite a lot about two men you only met last evening."

"Do I?"

"Which one of them got through to you?" the fair-haired girl inquired. "Not Burny, I'll bet— you'd only feel sorry for him. Gil, then?" Her lips curled. "Well, well. And we're even a little jealous, aren't we, because Jan knew him first."

Laura's sense of nausea wasn't exactly physical, although it made her suddenly push away her plate. The steak was cold anyway, and the salad had wilted. She couldn't see her own face, of course, but Jan could.

And Jan said, "Wait a minute, Sis. I'm sorry. I was only needling you. You know me."

"Unfortunately I do," Laura said, trembling. "A man with a great talent is practically helpless because you and Gil couldn't keep away from each other. At least Gil's accepted his share of the blame for what happened, but you—you don't even feel responsible for Burny, do you? Just sorry!"

"Listen. You think I wanted this to happen? It *happened*. One thing led to another, and we all got trapped. I hope to heaven you never have to find out how helpless that can make you feel. I can't undo anything, and I wouldn't go back to Burny even if I had the urge. Gil must be desperate for an idea. I ruined things for them before—why should I repeat?"

"Because Burny needs help," Laura told her.

"So *you* help him."

"I've tried to. I talked to Mr. Samuels at the Lodge. They've got a job there till the summer's over. They're opening tonight," Laura said.

"Good Lord," Jan muttered, staring across the

table at her. "That's fine. That's going to be cozy, isn't it?"

The clock over the kitchen stove had hummed its way past eight, Laura realized. That meant Gil and Burny were already playing in the Tavern Room, weaving their magic combination of guitar and piano.

There's still time to dress, she thought. Time to take the outboard and reach Lee's Landing and the Tavern Room, entranced and miserable and angry at such helplessness, asking herself why she had come and suspecting that where Gil Bricker was concerned, the lure might always be too strong to keep her away. Besides, Gil had asked her to be there for Burny's sake. That was enough reason, wasn't it?

Laura pushed back her chair with such a determined thrust that Phut-Phat leaped in fright and stood with his tail straight up and quivering.

"I've got a date," Laura announced, meeting her sister's questioning look.

"Tonight?" And for an instant Jan's eyes slid away toward the screen door and the waiting darkness of the woods. "I've been alone all day," she complained nervously. "Can't you stay in the first night I'm home?"

"I'll be back early," Laura told her coldly. "And don't lock me out again. Please."

But at the door she turned and for a moment looked at Jan with some of the old pain and perplexity. "Just tell me one thing, Jan. *Did* you steal that money?"

"I told you. I took it. I had to! But I'm not a thief. There's a difference!"

"Took it from whom?"

"From Harry Warrigal. But don't worry. He's so rich, he'll never miss it."

Chapter Seven

When Laura pushed open the driftwood door of the Tavern Room and let it sigh shut behind her, enveloping her in that underwater light and the murmur of a capacity crowd of well-behaved resorters, she was wearing high heels and a simple full-skirted black cotton.

It was as inconspicuous an outfit as she could put together, but it brought the usual reaction—off-center stares from the women close enough to turn an eye, and surreptitious attention from every man at the bar.

Recognizing her, a few of them spoke, but she moved on with a pleasant nod. Long ago she had discovered that it wasn't wise to mingle too casually with the guests at Lee's Landing. The wives were satisfied to let her teach their children how to swim, but they seemed to grow unhappy when she came into much contact with their husbands.

Besides, these people who could afford to vacation on the north shore of Talisman Lake were beyond her depth both socially and financially. And she suspected that they half considered her an employee.

She wasn't, of course, but it was tiresome to go around explaining that her father had once owned Lee's Landing and that she was simply part of the background.

She followed the curve of the bar where it ended against the wall and eased herself onto the padded stool, annoyed that her hands could reveal such a tremble as she lay her small black bag on the polished bar.

Less than ten feet away from her stood the ridiculous little piano where Gil had folded himself sidewise that afternoon, and the bar stool where Burny had perched like some sorrowful scarecrow. Both the piano and the stool were empty.

A small nerve coiled tighter in the pit of Laura's stomach. *What could have happened to them?* She glanced at her watch again, then once more across the smoke-hazed room. Had they simply failed to show up tonight after all the trouble she'd taken? Or had one of them got sick out on the island or been bitten by a snake or stumbled into poison ivy? Had they overturned themselves in the little craft that Mr. Samuels had loaned them?

She told herself her imagination was running wild. She was holding herself as stiffly as a stood-up date, her emotions running from apprehension to annoyance to bitterness. She told herself that she shouldn't have come here tonight. But she sat numbly and waited. Soon the bartender polished some space in front of her and deposited a napkin the size of a stamp.

"Well, Laura—I haven't seen you around here in weeks."

"I know. Early to bed and early to rise. It's the only way I can keep up with my kids."

"Can I get you something?"

"Just a coke. Plain," she added, a bid defensively.

"Why apologize?" His smile was weary. "It would be a good thing if more people drank plain cokes."

When he put the drink down in front of her, crisp with shaved ice, he said, "You'd better stick around. Mr. Samuels has hired something pretty special for the rest of the season. They're on a break now, but wait'll you hear these guys. Just a guitar and piano, but when they play, nobody breathes. Nobody even drinks. It's like Carnegie Hall."

She closed her eyes in relief. Then her heart shook as a sudden lift of applause greeted the two men returning to the spotlight. She could lean back against the wall and close her eyes again while Burny's guitar work sent its beat along every nerve ending.

Oh, she realized, they were with it tonight. Both of them. Gil with a dark and musing touch that matched his smile, while Burny sat hunched and listening at the crack of his own genius, tossing away those incredible chords as if they were confetti.

When another intense burst of applause made

Laura straighten up, she found Gil looking straight at her. Where she sat, the light was as dim as filtered twilight at the lake's bottom. She wondered if he had been searching for her. Whatever momentary surprise or pleasure might have crossed his square-cut features, she received only a noncommittal nod from him now. And then he leaned over to his blind partner and said something, and Burny turned to try to search for her.

But how could he? The black glasses started a sweep of the Tavern Room as if he was forcing himself to locate her without Gil's help—and her heart caught on an ache of pity, of affection. It was impossible not to feel rewarded for having come.

Again the two musicians leaned together and spoke, and after a moment Gil shrugged with a kind of irritatiton and slid out from his baby piano. Alone in the spotlight, Burny began to play something so devastatingly blue that any noise in the room would have been a sacrilege.

Laura, herself, was scarcely breathing, and she was unaware of Gil's approach until he edged onto the vacant stool beside her.

He held up two fingers, and the bartender quietly obliged him with a drink. She could feel his dark gaze across the rim of the glass. He keyed his voice for a private conversation.

"I thought you weren't going to come," he said.

"Obviously I changed my mind." She knew she sounded stiff. But with her eyes still on Burny, she said differently, "I'm glad I did. I'm glad I didn't miss this."

"He's doing it for you." And when her bewilderment showed, Gil explained. "The solo bit. When I told him you were here, he told me to clear out for a few minutes. It used to be a little habit he had. Wanting to take it alone when he felt good."

She didn't want to meet Gil's eyes again because it was impossible not to wonder how they'd often looked at Jan. Instead, imprinting circles on the bar with her glass, Laura said, "You sounded pretty good yourself a while ago."

"I was adequate," Gill said. He finished his drink and signaled for another.

"But with you, it's just a job."

"Is that bad? Knowing your own limitations?"

"I suppose not. But why become a piano player in the first place? Feeling like that."

"Because it happened. Doesn't everything—more or less?" Gil was staring into the curved mirror of the bar, but he was looking deeply at her. "I got to fooling around with the piano in high school, and then later I found I could make a living with it. I did a lot of things, from driving trucks in Alaska to raising chickens in Australia, but somehow when I was broke, I always wound up playing the piano somewhere. Anyway, pretty soon I decided to do my stint in the Army, and I ended up in West Berlin. That's where I met Burny. We were in communications together, but don't ask me why. Burny was just a

80

kid then—all red hair and elbows—and we all tried to mother him. We even helped him carry around that crazy guitar in a canvas sack." Gil half grinned. "After our discharge, he and I stuck together. He said I knew how to follow his beat."

"Until you wound up a little ahead of him," Laura said. "You and—and that girl."

"That's why he needs help now," Gil answered quietly. "From someone like you."

Burny had stopped playing. The applause itself seemed to isolate him, and Laura realized again that he was straining with some inner sense to locate her in the crowded room. With a sudden movement she left the bar and pushed her way through the fringe of people around his little clearing in the spotlight. And he knew she was there.

"Honey chick!" he said as his thin fingers reached out for her. "I knew I could play you out of hiding."

"Oh, Burny, you were wonderful!"

"I don't know. I could have topped it," he said, shifting his guitar so that he could pull her closer. "Stick around, will you? Please. We cut out at midnight. Gil says you won't listen to reason, but you've got to."

"It's no use," Gil told him patiently as he recramped himself under the piano. "I told you. I talked to her for an hour this afternoon."

"It's got to be use," Burny snapped back at him. "You want to let her throw away that voice without even trying?"

"What I want from her doesn't ring any bell," Gil said, running a clipped arpeggio with his big brown fingers.

Impulsively, Laura reached out and drew her fingers across the strings of Burny's guitar. She shouldn't have. They felt cold and razor sharp, and the discord was as unpleasant as the little shock of embarrassment that went through her.

People were looking at her. She was in the spotlight, holding up the entertainment, when she belonged back in a corner.

"Will you wait?" Burny demanded, his black glasses catching the light. "Then we'll try another session. Just for laughs."

"It will be funny, all right," Laura said.

"I didn't mean that."

"I know you didn't, Burny. All right," she sighed. "I have nothing else to do, I guess." She looked at Gil across the guitarist's sightless stare. "Just don't expect a miracle. And I'm not promising a thing," she added for Gil Bricker's benefit, half defying him, before she retreated to her corner of the bar.

When Gil and Burny started to weave their blue-hot patterns of jazz again, Laura forced herself to listen without a lift of emotion. She wondered if she really had a voice. Certainly not as good as Burny imagined, anyway. The whole idea simply refused to become real for her.

I'm a swimming teacher, she told herself, and she even had sore muscles to prove it. She was unused to such late hours, and fatigue was beginning to register. She had swum too hard that day, worried too much, pushed too strenuously against her own emotions.

Straightening her backbone, Laura extracted a compact from her bag, and her lipstick—a girl's sure defense against a complex world.

And at her elbow, a pleasant male voice said, "That's not your color. It should be a deep red. Very clear. Very subtle."

Against the uncertain light of the bar, she saw the pale crew cut first and then the impeccable cut of the gray jacket.

"Oh. Good evening," she said with an uncertain start. "Mr.—Mr.—"

"Lasher. Harrison Lasher. I don't see how you could forget me," he said, smiling. "I almost killed you this afternoon."

"I didn't recognize you without your dogs," she said, forcing a smile of her own.

"What are you drinking?"

"Coke. Very plain."

"How charming. Vodka Martinis," he ordered over one shoulder. "Two of them, buster. Imported vodka and very dry. Let's see if you can earn your tip." Then he said to Laura, "When you directed me to Lee's Landing this afternoon, why didn't you tell me you were staying here?"

"I'm not. I just work here."

"Work?"

"I work for myself," she said, wishing he were not leaning so close to her. "I teach swimming."

"Swimming? I never wanted to learn before. I enjoy judo, but no swimming." He picked up one of the double Martinis, and she found herself holding it.

"Do you give private lessons?" he asked.

"Well, yes—but—"

"How about one lesson a day? Starting tomorrow."

"Look—" she said coldly.

"I'd enjoy learning how to swim," he said. "If that's your business, why act as if I'd insulted you?"

"I'm not! It's just that I have so little free time. I—I'd have to look over my schedules—"

"Then look them over," he said, toying with his drink. "I don't expect to be here very long."

For some reason she bent her lips to the glass in her hand and even swallowed some of the vodka mixture. It tasted smooth and rather bitter—nothing to get worried about. Heat lifted into her cheeks without dissolving the little knot of excitement she felt. This man both intrigued and repelled her in a way that was tantalizing. She'd have to ask Mr. Samuels who he was. Where he came from. He was probably up to his ears in oil wells or uranium.

"By the way," Harrison Lasher said with an odd change of tone. "I hope you got rid of that cat."

"He's still as little as he was this afternoon,

which still doesn't make him a cat," she said. "And I'm keeping him."

She had the impression that a set of muscles worked thickly in Mr. Lasher's throat. Only an impression, because almost immediately he was smiling at her again.

"Cats are too sly and unpredictable. Like some women," he said. "Personally, I'd only trust a dog. You'll have to meet my two babies."

"Babies?" she echoed.

He laughed, his teeth very white. "Djong the Third of Canberra. And Wallah. You saw them in my car. The Canberra Kennel is a hobby of mine. They're a primitive breed, but very exceptional. They can be trained to a finer point than any man."

"A point of what?"

"Of obedience. Implicit," he said, and his heavy ring with the dog's head signet glittered as he turned a strong wrist and looked at his watch dial. "Which reminds me—it's time for their midnight run. I'm staying in Bungalow 10. Call me in the morning. After the lesson, I'll give you luncheon. Something special."

She was unable to free her tongue for any adequate protest until it was too late and he was gone. Mr. Harrison Lasher. She felt herself draw a deep breath and let it out slowly. Either she was exceptionally tired, or he had drained her last bit of vitality.

The idea of taking him on as a swimming pupil

was ridiculous, of course, although she could probably charge him fifty dollars an hour. It might deflate his ego a bit if she took him over his depth and left him to flounder.

Then again, he might end by besting her! There was a quality both unpredictable and domineering about him. At least he wasn't weak or dependent or in need of help from anyone. If he wanted to know her better, it was strictly for his own purposes. To a girl with a sore ego of her own, that was something.

And then she realized that it was past midnight.

While Gil stretched his muscles over the tiny piano, Burny tossed off a few melancholy chords that seemed to linger across the last movement of stragglers through the driftwood door.

When Gil came up to her, there were lines around his mouth and annoyance in his eyes.

"Burny wants to take you through a few songs. No problem. Just anything you know."

"Oh, Gil, do we have to? Can't we do it tomorrow instead?"

"Just long enough to humor him," Gil said. "Then we'll take you home."

But as she moved with dispirited compliance past him, Gil caught her arm. "Who was the joker with the platinum finish?"

"Mr. Lasher?"

"Who is he?" Gil repeated with chill patience. "I passed him in the lobby on one of our breaks and got a look I can still feel. Right in the back."

"Maybe he doesn't like jazz."

"That's all right with me."

"He's a guest here at the Lodge," she said.

"That ought to be chummy. What was all the yakking about?"

"Mostly about dogs and cats! Do you mind?"

"It's getting so I mind a lot about you," Gil said. His grip loosened, but his fingers still clung to her arm. "I resent men like that. They'll shoulder you off a broad sidewalk. Nobody counts but Number One."

"I might find that a novelty," she said.

"You also might find it a headache," Gil said, frowning into her flushed face. "I've seen that type operate before. Without the polish."

Chapter Eight

Burny, it turned out, was a hard-core perfectionist.

With the Tavern Room closed and midnight behind them, Burny had said, "Now just take it easy, Laura. Start singing anything you know—anything you like—and Gil and I'll back you up. No strain, see? Just for fun."

Hunched on the stool, with the focus of his black glasses never leaving her face, Burny was certainly a stranger to that listless and lethargic character Laura had saved from stepping off the cliff yesterday. He had become a patient but adamant slave-driver, without a sense of time or fatigue or of the impossibility of making her understand what he wanted from her.

"No," he'd snap out across a steel-sharp chord. "*No*, chick. Listen to the lyrics, will you? They're about love. About loneliness. Forget the tune and find the beat. You had it this afternoon for a while. O.K., man—let's take her through those last four bars again."

Her throat ached, her tongue was dry, and she had the feeling that a spell of nervous weeping might not be far away. If this was Gil's idea of humoring Burny, somebody was soon going to have to start humoring her.

"Listen, Burny. I can't," she said. "I just *can't*. I'm no singer, and I wouldn't want to be one if I could!"

Even Gil finally said, "Why don't you let up on her, Burny? This wasn't supposed to be a real rehearsal. I've had it myself. Do you know what time it is?"

"How would I know?" Burny murmured after a moment of warning stillness. "I haven't got a watch. If I had a watch, I couldn't see it. How would I know anything unless you were around to tell me?"

Oh no! Laura thought as her glance darted to Gil. *No. Not anything more tonight.* But Gil's face was quiet, and he said nothing.

Laura wondered if he understood. She tried to send him a smile of reassurance. Burny's flash of antagonism could only mean that he was beginning to resent his blindness and his dependence. It was a good sign. She wondered if Gil could see that he might be in for a lot of that if the change in Burny continued.

"I'm sorry," Gil said a bit stiffly to the man with the guitar. "You know I didn't mean—"

"Sure. Forget it. Like you said, we're all getting bushed," Burny admitted as he lifted the guitar from around his neck. "Anyway, you've really got what it takes," he said to Laura. "A couple more sessions like this, and I wouldn't be afraid to put you in the act."

She started to open her mouth, chewed the corner of it instead, and shot a look of angry help-lessness at Gil. This was getting out of hand, and even Gil looked less than happy about what he'd started. Yet his dark eyes were stubborn, and now there seemed to be no way to ease the atmosphere of strain between the two men.

It seemed wise to walk between them and to let Burny touch her own arm for guidance as they crossed the empty lobby of the Lodge and went out into the night.

The air was as hot and motionless as a blanket thrown around them, and the waning moon gave scant light as they followed the gravel walk that led down to the dock. Here and there, a pale path branched away to the darkened bunglaows.

And far off to the left—the faint howling of a dog had reminded her—sheltered against the woods that crowded in to separate Lee's Landing from the point on the north shore where her own cabin stood, was Bungalow 10.

The rent was appalling, she seemed to recall, and behind the walled patio was a tiny gem of a private pool. She didn't want to follow the train of association to Mr. Harrison Lasher himself, and she wondered why she had let it start in the first place.

When they reached the hooded floodlight on the dock, Gil pulled in one of the sleek little outboards that bore the Lodge's crest—no doubt the one that Mr. Samuels had loaned them. Laura ran a practiced eye over the aluminum craft. It seemed a bit racy for a bar-taught piano player to handle.

"Get in," Gil ordered after he had helped Burny step down. "We'll take you home."

"I'll take myself home, thanks. I can't leave my own boat here. I'll need it in the morning."

"Then we'll tie it on and tow it," Gil said irritably. "You're not wandering around alone at this hour."

"Listen. I've swum and sailed this lake more nights than you can count. I know it better than you know your own piano."

But she wasn't reluctant to obey him. The lake seemed distressingly empty and black. It was rather a relief to be wedged in securely between Gil and the wooden comfort of Burny's guitar. Only she shivered suddenly, strangely.

"Cold?" Gil asked her in understandable surprise.

"Just tired." And that howling dog somewhere. She wondered if it was in pain or only complaining at the moon?

Twenty minutes later Gil idled down the motor near the point and maneuvered the two boats quite deftly to a mooring where the black water chopped fretfully below Laura's pier. Above them at the edge of the woods, her cabin showed a single light.

Laura swallowed. Jan was still up! How stupid

91

to forget that she might be. But Jan surely wouldn't make the mistake of opening the front door.

Laura half wished that her sister would. It would be a fast finish, with no more complications to anything.

"Go ahead, Gil. Walk her up," Burny said as she climbed past his guitar. "We've got to take care of this girl. She's going to make us all famous."

It was useless for Laura to protest to either man that she didn't need an escort up to her own cabin. She tried and then she stopped trying, and when Gil tucked her elbow securely against him and started up the reed-edged path in the darkness, a lethargy of yearning fell over her.

She knew that she should hurry, should say good night. What was the use of hoping that Gil might use this brief moment alone together to say something that mattered? That mattered about *them?*

A hundred feet above them, her cabin still betrayed that single light, but no door opened, no petulant voice from Jan called down to inquire about Laura's lateness.

Like a sagging balloon, the last quarter-moon seemed to cast a green shadow over the lake where Burny had taken to his guitar again. The sound of his playing seemed to rise from strings barely touched.

Laura felt Gil's steps slowing her down. And

when she halted, she felt herself tremble. Was it possible to open up just a little private truth between them? Apparently not.

Gil said, "You know Burny's right. If you're willing to sweat your heart out, you can probably make it. Fame. Money. A career up the ladder."

"I don't care. I don't want it! But even if I did, you'd expect me to be grateful to him, wouldn't you?"

"I don't know. I suppose so. At least I'm grateful to you."

"So you've told me."

"It wouldn't help to tell you anything more."

"Because of Burny." She was bitter now.

"Because he's blind and it's my fault. Can't you understand that? He's got to come first, and I've got to know I'm doing everything I can. I've got to *know* that," Gil repeated harshly. "That's why I brought him here to Talisman Lake. That's why I wanted to find that girl. But Jan isn't important any more—I realized that tonight. If you'll just stick with him for a while, that may be all he needs. And you won't be hurting yourself."

"Have you any idea what you sound like?" Laura said to him.

"I know what I sound like. It doesn't matter. Burny can't see. *That's* what matters."

"And we don't. I mean, not much."

"We can't," Gil said.

She felt herself smiling. "All right. But you ought to stop doing so much penance. You're not entirely to blame, are you, and you can't change the past. Why don't you stop meddling with the future? Why don't you stop trying to tidy up Burny's life? What right have you to dismiss one girl, then try to push in another? Suppose I hurt him, too? What then?"

"You wouldn't. You're not like that."

"But I'm human, and so I Burny," Laura said on a shortened laugh, wondering if her relationship with Jan would damn her by association if he knew. "That might complicate the problem if I let him turn me into a singer. You might even have to start salvaging things all over again."

What Gil did was to reach out and take her in his arms. Her voice had risen, and perhaps he couldn't quiet her in any other way. It was no answer, though. It was a kind of delusion with a half-sick letdown. She clung and wanted him to let her go.

What separated them was a sound—a sound that went on and on, an animal sound that set Gil's fingers into her like clamps.

Above them at the edge of the woods, something crashed and whined and tore at something else. A scream of agony was ripped from some smaller creature. There was a crashing through the underbrush, then a silence so thick that Laura could barely hold herself erect beneath its pressure.

Chapter Nine

From down below them on the lake, Burny cried, "Gil? Laura? Are you all right? What happened, for God's sake?"

"I'm not sure. But we're O.K.," Gil called back. It must have been some kind of an animal. A wildcat, maybe."

Laura said, "No one's seen a wildcat around here for years. And it couldn't have been a bear—we're too far down state. But whatever it was—" she swallowed—"it must have killed something."

"I'd better have a look," Gil said.

"No—wait! I—I don't want to know."

But he left her, anyway.

The red and dormant moon had slipped behind some clouds now, leaving barely enough predawn starlight for her to see him moving about at the edge of the woods on a level with her cabin. From his movements, he seemed to bend down and throw something far off into the trees. She heard the faint crash of its landing. Not *Phut-Phat!* she prayed. *Not that wisp of royal kittenhood!*

Her hand lay against her throat. Then suddenly

she felt something spurt playfully from the reeds and take a swipe at her ankle.

"Phut-Phat!" she sobbed, snatching up the baby Siamese. "Shame on you—cavorting around like an old Tom. Who let you out at this hour, anyway?"

She knew the answer to that. Jan had probably put the tiny thing out hours ago and forgotten him. It was just like her, irresponsible even with a kitten. Laura's anger and alarm were still drumming in her when Gil returned.

He said, "Whatever it was, it ripped out half the bushes. I'm not sure what it killed—a rabbit, maybe—there wasn't much left." And his oddly tight voice added, "But it dropped this."

Her puzzled gaze left his face and went down to the object gleaming faintly on his palm. "What is it?" she said.

"What does it look like?"

She was staring at it stupidly, but obviously it was a platinum cigarette case, wafer-thin, bearing a dog's head signet in diamonds.

Her voice was uncertain. "It must belong to Harrison Lasher. It matches his ring. And that animal—it must have been one of his dogs."

"Nice dogs," Gil said. "They like to visit you?"

His eyes were extremely dark. Meeting them again, Laura said, "What is that supposed to mean? I barely know the man, and I don't like his dogs." She put out her hand to him. "Gil—"

But he pushed the platinum case into it. "You'll

want to return this," he said. "But tell Lasher he'd better keep his dogs chained. They're liable to chew off your leg."

After Laura had closed the cabin door behind her, she stood listening as the purr of Gil's outboard faded across the lake toward Spider Island. She felt plagued by an angry loneliness. Should she have tried to explain the dogs and the cigarette case? As she moved heavily to snap on another lamp, she wondered if she could have explained it.

Of course, the case had been dropped by accident. When? When Harrison Lasher had been giving his "babies" their midnight run? He had even taken leave of her in the Tavern Room for that very purpose. But why the time lapse of several hours if those had been his dogs? And the distance from Lee's Landing to the point suggested more of a purposeful hike across the heavily wooded terrain than a leisurely run for his pets.

He must have gotten lost, she decided. He must have wandered into the woods behind his bungalow and become confused enough to tramp about for hours. She hadn't told him where she lived, so his reaching her cabin must have been accidental. Perhaps he had dropped his cigarette case hours ago, after all. He surely couldn't have been near when one of his dogs made that atrocious kill in the darkness.

Laura had half expected to find Jan cowering in a corner, panicked by the sounds of movement and violence around the cabin. Instead, Laura found her in bed, asleep—unbelievably asleep in her cluttered bedroom after all that commotion outside.

Laura stifled a giggle, and knew it was from nerves. She'd better get to bed herself.

But a few bleak hours later, when they faced each other across the breakfast table, Laura felt neither hysterical nor relieved, nor even slightly tolerant of his sister's uncombed hair and her rumpled pajamas and the untidy robe that hung off her shoulders.

"Don't you ever get dressed?" Laura snapped, pouring herself a blissfully black cup of coffee.

Her mood was almost murderous. She had slept hardly at all. The sunlight felt like a drill against her eyes; a heavy schedule of swimming classes lay ahead; and just beyond the edge of her headache lay the problem of Harrison Lasher.

She could feel the weight of his cigarette case in the pocket of her skirt. When she returned it, he'd probably explain. The possibility of explaining anything to Gil Bricker, however, was simply too much. She couldn't even face the thought of it until the coffee started working.

"What do you care how I look?" Jan said sulkily, pushing back her silk-gold hair. "You promised to get home early last night, and you didn't. You've hardly been here since I came. A few more days of this and I'll flip!"

"Then why don't you leave?"

"I thought I'd explained that."

"You've explained little, Jan, except that I'm to keep quiet about your being here. Well, I can't do it much longer. Gil and Burny brought me home last night. Gil might show up here again. What am I supposed to do them?"

"Invite him in," Jan suggested as she leaned over to help herself to her sister's coffee. I can handle Gil if I have to. Only you're not keen about that, are you?"

Jan's eyes held a glint of mockery as she sipped the steaming brew, but then the light went out, leaving her face looking very young as she said, "I'm sorry, Sis. I ruin everything I touch these days And you haven't got a prayer with Gil—not if he finds out we're sisters."

"Then go away. I mean it," Laura said with difficulty, leaning both hands hard on the breakfast table. "You've got all that money. Can't you take it and go far away someplace? I don't want to sound unkind. I'd help you if I knew how. But this is impossible!"

"So is going away," Jan mumbled. She was pale, and her eyes clung like a child's. There was a look about her straight out of their childhood as she added, "It's no use. This is the end of the line for me. If Harry Warrigal finds me, I'm dead, that's all. Just dead."

For a moment that seemed unending, Laura could only stand over the breakfast table, the early morning sunlight bright on the pottery dishes, her sister's words hanging between them.

"Surely you must be joking." Laura breathed at last, meeting Jan's pleading stare.

"I'm not. I'll be dead. Harry will kill me himself if he can find me. Or worse! He's the man who had Burny beaten up by mistake! The one I was going to marry—"

"I know, I know," Laura whispered, and sank onto the edge of her chair. "But you said he was wealthy—important—that the money wouldn't matter—" and Laura shook her head in confusion. "You must be imagining things. He might want to have you arrested, but no sane person would—"

"Harry isn't sane," Jan said shrilly. "I told you that. He's vicious and he's crazy, and none of it shows on the outside. I didn't know that at first. He's not even human. He enjoys destroying people with fear—watching them suffer and crawl. He'd deliberately make me drink too much until I'd make a fool of myself or start to cry; then he'd sit beside me and tell me I'd better change after we were married or he'd be forced to do something unpleasant.

"He said I was beautiful but ignorant. He'd smile and say it was going to be interesting, having a wife to train. It was a game with him. He's like someone you read about and never believe exists. He told me once that if I ever tried to leave him, he'd ruin my looks forever."

On a sob, Jan muttered, "I'd have left him anyway, but I couldn't! There was no way, Laura! I told you—he was always watching me. Or somebody was. Then one day in Miami we were having luncheon in his office in the hotel when he got a phone call. He said he'd be back in an hour and that I'd better be packed and waiting. We were going to Jamaica, he said, to close some kind of a deal. We'd be married down there and turn the rest of the trip into a honeymoon. A honeymoon! He meant a jealousy-ridden nightmare."

Jan's fingers fumbled with a cigarette, and the first heavy puff on it seemed to calm her a bit. Then, through a cloud of gray smoke, she continued. "When he was gone, I prowled around the office like I was suffocating. Then I remembered the wall safe. All I wanted was just enough money to help me get away. God knows why he'd forgotten to flip the combination. I think I'd have broken into it with my fingernails if I'd had to. I just grabbed what came first—I thought it was only a few hundred dollars, and I didn't stop to count it. Then I simply walked out the back entrance. It was like a dream. I don't know why nobody stopped me. I walked to the nearest bus station and bought a ticket and climbed on a bus.

"I felt as if I'd been drugged or beaten on the head. I wasn't even trying to plan what next or where to go. When the bus reached Toledo, I stayed in a cheap rooming house. I was sick. It was nerves, I guess, but then I caught the flu besides. Then one day the landlady said she thought someone was watching my room. I thought I couldn't get out of bed, but I made it. Then I thought of you—of the lake here—how peaceful and pretty it used to be. I got away from him again, Laura, but if Harry ever finds me—!

Her beautiful face looked shadowed and sunken to the bones, without passion or complaint now, only the slim eyes of a far-gone childhood betraying the core of her desperation. Yet all at once she shrugged and fixed a smile in place.

"It isn't because I took his money," she explained. "I've seen Harry lose more than that on a dull day at the races. It's because I walked out on him and got away with it. Nobody does things like that to Harry Warrigal. He's an egomaniac."

She laughed then, and picked up the kitten at her feet, and tickled its ears with gentle affection.

Laura studied her with a feeling hopelessness and despair. Could anyone who was close to Jan, even though sickened by the frightening and stupid things she had done with her life, fail to be drawn to her for that very delinquency of heart that gave her such defiance and appeal? No wonder Gil had been in love with her once. And Burny, too.

And was Jan entirely to blame? She'd had an older sister to guide her, to bring her up. How far back *did* responsibility go? Laura wondered heavily.

She gazed in futility at the uneaten breakfast, then at her watch. It was past nine o'clock.

"Jan, I've got to go,," she said. "I've got four classes this morning. I don't know what to say to you. It's so—so awful. But maybe you ought to go to the police. Or send the money back to this man. That might help, mightn't it?"

"And give Harry that much satisfaction? I don't want a cent of it, but I'll burn it first! Besides, if I can stay here, I don't think he'll be able to find me. He doesn't know my name was ever Jenny Brown. He never bothered about where I came from, and I never told him."

"Are you sure?" Laura murmured, remembering how frightened Jan had been the day she arrived.

"Certainly I'm sure."

Jan said. "Talisman Lake is two thousand miles from Miami, and I never even mentioned the place to him."

"You might have," Laura answered slowly. "You mentioned it to Gil Bricker once. If Gil could trace you here, why can't this Harry Warrigal?"

Chapter Ten

The morning sky was as pale as a robin's egg but the lake gave back a flash of steel as Laura headed her slim red craft toward Lee's Landing.

She glanced down at her clipboard and the familiar beach bag. Ordinary things! It was becoming just a bit difficult to remember there was an ordinary world where most people lived in relative quiet and dullness.

A pain in her hands made Laura realize that she was gripping the red wheel so hard that her fingernails were curved back deep into the palms. *"I've got to calm down she told herself. Jan must have exaggerated. She's been sick and nervous. Frightened for weeks.*

Jan was in trouble, yes, but surely not in physical danger from this man.

Harry Warrigal. That name alone! It sounded odd and ugly, as if he might have a gun bulging beneath his coat. Apparently, though, he hadn't. Just enough money and personality to blind a little fool like her sister until it had been too late. But would a man such as Jan had described spend his time tracking down a fiancée who had helped herself to his petty cash and then disappeared, when he could no doubt find dozens of other girls to marry him? He might, Laura realized, if he was a real psychopath, for Jan's disappearance could have dealt an intolerable blow to his unbalanced ego.

It hurt to have to think of her sister in such a vicious predicament, but at least Jan had been honest. Laura suddenly had a picture of herself again —neither wise nor responsible enough to have prevented Jan's leaving home in the first place. But Jan *must* have exaggerated about the danger— she'd always been too emotional and suggestible. And sooner or later she was certain to become fed up with her own self-imposed isolation and leave Talisman Lake, Laura decided as she cut her tiny craft toward shore.

The thing to do was to mark time and help her sister if she could and not let herself be drawn into these eddies of fear. And not lie to Gil if he ever discovered the relationship between them. She'd keep quiet because she had to, because she'd reluctantly promised Jan that she could remain hidden in the cabin. But she wouldn't lie to Gil.

With a resolute jerk on the line, Laura tied up at the dock and went in search of her first beginners' class of the morning. She was inexcusably late, but where were her five youngsters?

Shading her eyes, she scanned the shore line right and left to the wood's edge, then back along the shallow water and up across the flowered lawns to the Lodge, its glass front gleaming like a show window in the sunlight.

A few people sat on the terrace over late breakfast or moved toward the festively striped cabanas to oil and sun themselves. It was all quite normal except for the absence of her tadpoles.

After another ten minutes, Laura started in perplexity for the Lodge. She was heading for the resort phone in the lobby when Mr. Samuels emerged from his office.

"Oh. Laura. I was just going down to the dock to find you."

"I'm afraid I'm late," she said. "So late, my first class has vanished. I thought I'd better phone their parents and check up."

"That won't be necessary. I've phoned them for you. I know it's a bit irregular, but as a matter of fact I've canceled all your lessons this morning. I'm sure you can arrange to have them made up."

"I can? I certainly hope so. Do you mind telling me why?"

"Because we have a new guest. A Mr. Harrison Lasher from Chicago. It was he who suggested that I clear the morning for you. He said you'd arranged a private lesson for him and that he'd prefer not being rushed through it. I'm afraid I couldn't very well refuse." Mr Samuels coughed and straightened his tie.

Laura said, "That's odd, Mr. Samuels. Especially since I'm not an employee here."

"Yes. Well. No need to sound like that, Laura. I

106

seem to remember doing you a favor for those two musicians. And as I said—what I did was irregular, but Mr. Lasher happens to be an important stockholder in the resort association that owns us. I thought it best to cooperate. I'm sure you understand."

"Of course," she said with a stiff smile. "But Mr. Lasher is mistaken about the lesson. I found something that belongs to him though, so I might as well return it."

"Fine," Mr. Samuels said with relief. "He's in Bungalow 10. I believe he's waiting for you."

When Laura reached the door of Bungalow 10, set close against the woods in expensive seclusion, its private pool and patio hidden behind a fieldstone wall that was itself concealed by shrubbery, she found herself jabbing at the doorbell and then taking an uncertain step backwards. Braced, she caught her breath when the door opened, only to let it slide away in temporary relief.

A dark-skinned houseboy in a jacket as crisp as a glacier bestowed a grin of delight upon her.

"Miss Laura Brown?"

"Miss Laura Brown."

"Come in, please. Mr. Lasher says please wait by pool. Very cool. Very pleasant. Mr. Lasher on telephone. Very important call long distance."

It seemed an even longer distance across the elegance of the split-level bungalow and out into ordinary sunlight again.

Blinking at the contrast, Laura let her gaze

move across the high-walled enclosure where the surface of the pool sparkled with a pale brilliance. The studied setting included two beach lounges, plus a table set with silver and linen beneath the shade of a canopy. She realized it was impossible to remain indifferent to the effect that had been created for her benefit.

Lying slack-necked on the nearest lounge were Harrison Lasher's sand-colored dogs. The pair of them were unchained, she noticed at once, and when she stopped dead, their heads came erect, but their eyes fastened on her with indiffernece.

"You like dogs?" inquired the houseboy, who had reappeared with a frosted drink the color of overripe persimmons in a glass as thin as a tube.

"I like some dogs," she said, still eyeing the immobile animals.

"These dogs very special breed called dingoes. Come from Australia. Very well trained. Never bark. Never bite. Never move unless Mr. Lasher says."

"That's nice. Then they wouldn't kill anything unless Mr. Lasher says."

The houseboy looked so startled, she had to reassure him. "I mean kill rabbits, perhaps."

"Oh, hunt!" he exclaimed with his vast grin. "Dogs hunt very well. Hunt anything Mr. Lasher orders."

And from the doorway, the crew-cut Mr. Lasher explained pleasantly, "Even human beings. I mean, dingoes could be trained to hunt criminals or an enemy in wartime. I doubt if even a pair of them could actually kill a man, but they could slash him so badly he might wish they had." And with a soft snap of his fingers, he murmured, "Djong! Wallah! Come, babies."

The cup-eared babies melted off the lounge and padded off like hypnotized wraiths into the bungalow.

"Well, Miss Brown. Laura, isn't it? Laura," he said, with his peculiar light-eyed smile, "I was wondering what kept you."

He was wearing gray swimming trunks and a terrycloth robe as thick as a storm cloud. His waist was flat, his chest superb.

Laura met his eyes and said, "Nothing kept me. I don't like having my classes canceled, either. I thought I'd already explained, Mr. Lasher—I work for myself."

"Congratulations. So few of us can. I also understand that your father once owned this resort site. He was able to leave you a deserted island, but nothing else. You had a rather wild sister who left home three years ago, and since then you've lived by yourself. You're twenty-three, unattached, and you have a charitable heart. Samuels was kind enough to fill me in pretty thoroughly on you. But it didn't seem to surprise him that a girl with your beauty hasn't bettered herself before now. It does me."

"That's one of the hazards of my work," she said. "Tiresome questions. Look, Mr. Lasher.

Shall we get to the point? I simply have no time to give you swimming lessons."

"I doubt that. I'm sure I can afford to pay whatever you ask. Even more."

"It's not a question of money." She was hot-cheeked, curt, and inadequate. "I'm booked up for the season."

"I doubt that too," he said. "I think you've decided I'm a menace—the way I almost ran you down the other day."

"Of course not. It was nothing. I—I mean—"

"Well, there's no hurry about the lessons. And perhaps I can make you change your mind. But why don't you relax and try your drink," he suggested, putting just enough pressure on her elbow to move her toward the nearest lounge at the pool's edge. "It's something special I picked up in Puerto Rico."

The tube of glass was so cold, her fingers ached from the contact, and when she put the pink liquid to her lips, she was surprised that any drink could taste so sweet and bland when its after-taste was so tainted.

"Don't you like it?"

"I'm afraid not!" she gasped. "It's so—odd."

"Try it again," he said, standing over her. "A person has to become conditioned to odd things—"

Suddenly, the muscles in his throat seemed to close on a spasm. His smile became a grimace because his eyes went blank.

She was about to get to her feet, when the look vanished. She wondered if it had been some sort of physical seizure, or a trick of the sunlight reflected on the pool. Her heart was beating thickly. She could have imagined it—he had such an unsettling effect on her.

She felt him remove the glass from her fingers. "You'd better work up to these gradually," he said. "And you don't drink—I'd forgotten that. I'll have my boy fix you something else."

"No. Please. I can't stay," she whispered. "I only wanted to return this."

She fumbled and almost dropped the platinum case. It flashed like a wafer of fire.

She had to ask him, "It's yours, isn't it?"

"What makes you think so?"

"The signet matches your ring," she said, turning it over.

"Your're not only beautiful, but observant. Also honest," he said with a relaxed movement as he accepted the platinum trifle and slipped it into the pocket of his robe. "I hadn't even missed it."

"You dropped it near my cabin on the point last night."

"Your cabin?" And the faintest pause held him while he frowned. "I wish I'd known that," he said. "I'd have stopped in to ask for directions. I must have wandered around for hours before I had sense enough to follow the shore line back. Djong had slipped his chain, and I had a devil of a time collaring him again. He was onto a scent. A cat, probably. He hates them as much as I do."

"It wasn't a cat, but he made enough noise killing it."

"And he frightened you, didn't he?"

Again his eyes went blank. The dogs reappeared on silent pads to drop at their master's feet. He reached out with his foot and scratched the female, Wallah, on the flank. The dog quivered and let her tongue hang out on the hot tiles.

The man's smile came back slowly and with a great deal of charm. "We keep getting off on the wrong foot. I wonder why," he said. "You surely must be used to having men find you attractive and wanting to know you better. However—I seem to have caused you a lot of inconvenience one way or another. The least I can do is give you a good lunch."

"Thanks, but no," she mumbled.

"I want you to stay, Laura."

"I'd like to, but I have another engagement," she lied.

"With whom?" he asked. "With the one named Gil or the one named Burny?"

Djong slit his eyes at her and yawned, showing teeth like thick white thorns. The pool rippled noiselessly under a soft breeze, and the ivy moved on the high wall.

She said, "Is there anything Mr. Samuels forgot to tell you, I wonder?"

"Jazz musicians. Samuels said you picked them

up somewhere and brought them to him for a job. I heard them last night." He grimaced.

"You don't have to like hot jazz. It isn't compulsory."

"He said he hired them as a favor to you. I expect he could also fire them," Harrison Lasher told her with regret.

Chapter Eleven

The sun was beginning to slant across the early sky of afternoon before Laura left Bungalow 10 and wandered slowly back down to the lake shore. Relaxed fingers swung her beach bag. She moved in an afterglow of pleasure, with her mind still somewhat blank. She felt puzzled but well fed.

That luncheon! She remembered it blissfully. Served behind the ivied wall by Mr. Lasher's houseboy, it had been sheer perfection. A cold chicken aspic the color of sunlight, piping hot rolls no larger than walnuts, and the most delicious coffee she had ever tasted. Iced, with a dollop of cream on top. Dessert would have been as superfluous as was her former fear of Harrison Lasher.

She was uncertain now whether Mr. Lasher himself had actually intimidated her into staying or only charmed her. He had made that mild remark that Mr. Samuels would be able to remove Gil and Burny from their nightly stint in the Tavern Room, and he had expressed a dislike for hot jazz, but then he had started to talk about something else—his ranch in Nevada, and deep-sea fish-

114

ing off the Florida Keys. Then he had made his dogs do tricks for her. No host could have been more considerate or entertaining. It would have been boorish to walk out on him, and then somewhere along the afternoon, she hadn't wanted to at all.

She still wasn't sure what his business interests were except resort property and the breeding of dingoes, but he was certainly attractive and hardminded. And wealthy. As she lifted her gaze to the empty island across the lake, she wondered if it was wrong to let herself be impressed by such qualities. At least he was vastly different from other men she had met.

Sighing, she turned onto the dock, and saw a stranger sitting on the red-padded seat of her motorboat.

What fooled her momentarily was the absence of the black glasses. The man didn't fasten them on until he heard her step, and then a welcoming grin lighted up his face like a lamp. Somebody must have taken a scissors to his hairline. It was shorter, although still ragged as an owl's. "Burny! For goodness' sake, how long have you been here?"

"Long enough to get a sunburn. What kept you?"

"A swimming lesson I didn't give. There was a little—confusion."

"Well, I figured something like that. Gil checked around for you and said I'd better not wait. I said I'd wait anyway. We argued. He's bugged, that man. Something's at him. I said just park me in your boat. What have I got but time?"

She watched him slide his strong, thin fingers along the polished gunwale. It wouldn't have surprised her to hear music rise from his touch.

"This is a real nervous boat," he said with respect.

"Burny—you mean you can—"

"Don't chew your lip, honey. No, I can't see the boat. Or can I? I don't know," he said, with movement of intensity and irritation. "I keep feeling if I just try hard enough—" His bony shoulders shrugged. He seemed to stare up at her. "Anyway, it's bright, isn't it?"

"It's red. You make a perfect pair," she said, climbing down beside him. "How about a fast ride to Conover's? We'll get some cokes."

"Nah. That's where Gil went load up on groceries for us. Let's split to the island."

"The island?"

"Another session," Burny explained, patting the guitar that rested against his leg. "Gil chewed me out for working you too hard last night, so I thought we'd take it easier today."

"What about Gil? No piano," she reminded Burny, gripping the wheel.

"We don't need either of them. We can work through some numbers just for the beat. I want you to relax and get with me. Then we'll have a sound I've always dreamed about."

116

After a moment she put her hand out for the starter. What could you do with a blind man who sounded this eager? She took her pressures out on the boat, whipping it across open water like a jet, spreading a white and angry wake behind them as she turned down along the inhospitable shoreline of Spider Island. She wanted to blame Gil for this ridiculous idea, but she couldn't quite do it.

She kept one eye out for the rotting old pier stuck in the reeds and muck, but just how was she supposed to lead Burny past the cliff to their campsite by the cove?

For an instant, his disability filled her with hot annoyance. He was like a spoiled child—everyone humoring him. Poor Burny. Who else mattered? And then she saw the way he was holding himself, helpless in her hands because she might run them into a stone wall, his face blank and stiff with waiting. Shame flooded her as she throttled down.

He said, "You can go in at the cove. Gil rigged a dock."

It was such a rough but solid job, extending from the rocky tip of the cove into water deep enough to clear the propellers of any lake craft, that she exclaimed, "Burny, this is perfect! But how did he do it in such a short time?"

"He ought to belong to the carpenters' union. Anything with his hands and muscles. Sometimes I wonder why he sticks to the piano."

"Perhaps because of you," she said, uncertain

about helping him onto the dock. "I mean, because you make such a wonderful team."

"Do we?" Burny said as he stumbled, then banged his guitar on one of Gil's pilings. "He's got a good solid style and I like working with him, but I could get somebody else. Gil's not indispensable. Even to a blind man."

Laura had expected to meet a natural resentment occasionally, but not this. The bitterness in Burny's outburst shocked her. She wondered if he had been carrying it aound for a long time, hidden behind the lethargy.

And she shared Burny's bitterness. Gil was such a fool, persuading and half plaguing her into this —into letting Burny believe he could make a singer out of her and give her a career she simply did not want. She loved jazz, but not to perform it. She loved elephants, but she didn't want a trunk.

"You don't know what this means to me, Laura," Burny was saying. "The whole pattern—just finding you. I keep thinking about the things we can do together if we're willing to work."

"Burny—please—you shouldn't be so sure," she whispered.

"I am sure. You've got it. All the way." His black glasses glittered in the slanting sun. "I wish I could see you," he said. "Sometimes I think I can. Like the dark was going to crack open any second and you'd be there."

A soft pain held her motionless as Burny

touched her face, his fingers thin and warm and electric as they traced her features.

"Gil says you're too beautiful."

"I'll bet!"

"What do you mean by that?"

"Oh, I don't know."

She moved away from him along the sandy beach, struggling against a misery that drained her. She suddenly wished that she could block out both these men and be back with Harrison Lasher. He wasn't weak and he didn't need anything. He hadn't wanted her to leave after their luncheon together by the pool, and she wished now, with an abrupt violence, that she had stayed.

Behind her, Burny said, "I think I ought to tell you something. Gil and I had some trouble over another girl."

Laura's heart caught. She said carefully, "It doesn't matter, Burny."

"Maybe Gil's told you already, but I think you ought to hear my version. She worked in the same night club with us. She was blonde and beautiful as a dream, and I fell pretty hard. But it ended fast when *this* happened to me. Gil keeps calling it my 'accident'—like he was treading on eggs. Accident, hooey. I just got mugged in an alley one night. I landed in the hospital, but this girl never came near me. Not a word, not a line. Well, I had a lot of time, lying there with my head in a bandage, and I got to thinking. I figured it out. The reason she didn't want to see me was because she and Gil had tumbled for each other. I used to wonder if there wasn't something between them. I don't say it was all his fault. She was hard to ignore. But that's the way it added up to me. He took her away from me when I was flat on my back. When I couldn't even see."

"So you decided to give up and stay that way?" Laura asked him, staring into his grim and sightless face.

"It was a rotten trick."

"Why didn't you tell Gil how you felt? Why didn't you *talk* about it?"

"I didn't want to talk. It was a rotten trick," Burny repeated sullenly. "Anyway, by then I was helpless and Gil had started hovering around me like a mother hen."

Laura started to speak, but the effort faded. She wanted to tell him something, but he probably couldn't have understood. She was no psychologist, she was only trying to feel it out with her heart; but it seemed plain to her now why Burny hadn't regained his sight. Unconsciously, he was punishing Gil. His false blindness had nothing to do with having loved or lost Jan, as Gil thought. It had been an infantile and devious reaction toward a stronger man whom Burny had probably both looked up to and been jealous of. And it had been completely unconscious. That was the pity of it.

The doctors could have thought it through more clearly, she realized, but somehow she knew she was right. And still she was unable to help him.

120

With a sense of defeat she said, "Perhaps it wasn't Gil's fault or the girl's. You shouldn't have withdrawn so much, Burny. Or maybe it just happened."

But Burny's version was near enough to the truth. Why fill him in on the whole miserable mess? Gil would still rationalize the guilt he carried, and Burny would still walk around like a sulky adolescent with suspicions eating into him. They were both right and dreadfully wrong.

"You may be right, but it'll never happen again," Burny said slowly. "The next time I get serious about a girl, my bighearted buddy had better keep strictly away."

Hours passed.

Laura tilted her head and watched a flight of birds sweep in low over Talisman Lake and then mount on a curve that carried them high over the cliff where she and Burny sat, and then down into the silent woods behind. She closed her eyes and the pink clouds of sunset vanished. Her throat felt like flannel, but Burny didn't belive in taking breaks. Or he had forgotten that anyone could tire.

She wondered how long they had been working, repeating a phrase a hundred times, following a rhythm down where the blues became a subtle communion between nerves and music.

It was fortunate—or unfortunate!—that she had spent so many lonely and entranced hours with a record collection that contained so much of the best—vocalists from the incomparable Bessie Smith up to the exciting newcomers on little-known labels. She must have been absorbing jazz lyrics for years, because there didn't seem to be anything—bop or ballad, old or new—that she couldn't slide into once Burny had set the beat.

It was uncanny too—as if another self sang while she watched in bewilderment and disapproval. Sometimes when Burny had grinned, she had felt a moment's thrill of accomplishment, but the session had taken a lot out of her.

She moved irritably, her glance following a sailboat that danced across the lake. She couldn't understand why Gil hadn't shown up. How could it take him this long to return from Conover's Store with supplies?

Her face was still turned toward the empty lake when she heard Burny improvise a bit of swing that ended on a chord of finality, so tense and off-beat, it was like a slap.

"Well, how about that? You still think you can't dig it?" he said, easing the guitar from around his neck at last.

"I still think I'm dreaming. Whoever heard of a rehearsal like this? Sitting on a rock on a deserted island, warbling to the birds. I thought you had to have a cellar somewhere, plugged up with liquor fumes and cigarette smoke."

"You've got to have the talent and the urge. You and I could kick it anywhere, Laura. Any time," he said, a line of sweat showing beneath the glasses that held her in their black intensity.

She paused to let him grip her arm as they started back down the steep and pebbled slope. But his hand suddenly slid around her and she was against him.

"Just stick with me, will you, Laura? I don't ask for much. Just you and a guitar and a couple of right breaks."

He was rough, and he frightened her. No wonder he had once been tagged with such a name. He was burning again, but his new vitality seemed charged with unreason.

She said quietly, "Burny, I don't want to be a singer. Not professionally."

"You're crazy. With that voice?"

"I know you think I am. But can't we just—well, not be so serious about this thing? I've got a job already. I like it, and I live here. This is my home, Burny, and I'm not very ambitious."

He rubbed his hand across his mouth, and then he laughed. "Wait till I put you in front of a mike sometime. With an audience. You'll thank me."

They stumbled and slid down the slope together, and walked close on the overgrown path. When they reached the cove, there was still no Gil.

Laura walked to the collar of beach and felt the sand turning chill. The lake had darkened beneath a flushed sky that promised the deepness of evening. She wanted to think and she wanted to get away. But how could she leave Burny alone on the island?

"Where is that dumb joker?" Burny demanded as he stumbled over a camp chair. "He's got the family watch—why doesn't he use it? The sun's down, isn't it?"

"Not quite. But something must have happened. Maybe he ran out of gas."

"Wouldn't you know it? He's been yapping for weeks about getting back to work. Getting *me* back to work. So now we've got a spot, he's going to make us late the second night."

There was nothing to do finally but run Burny and his guitar back to the Lodge, and then settle him in one of the booths in the Tavern Room.

"What time is it?" he demanded.

"After seven."

"Many people yet?"

"Well, it's filling up. But don't worry. I'll find Gil. He could have developed engine trouble."

"So what? Who needs him? I've played plenty of solos before."

Laura realized that that was probably true. The first time she had heard Burny play, it was the half-savage loneliness of his music that had drawn her to the island. He couldn't do less than entrance any group of listeners.

She said, "I'll circle the island again, then check over at Conover's. Maybe he's stalled somewhere. There could even have been an accident."

"So he's stalled," Burny said. "So we make some changes. I meant what I said—who needs him?"

"Now wait a minute—" she breathed as she looked at him.

"For what? Gil's permission?" He reached up quite accurately for her arm and pulled her in beside him. He said, "Listen. You know how I learned to swim when I was kid? Somebody gave me a shove into the East River. It scared me silly, but I swam. I'll scare you too, but you'll sing."

"I won't. You said I was crazy, but you are! This isn't amateur night, Burny."

"You don't sing like an amateur."

"I don't sing at all! If I opened my mouth in front of all these people, I'd choke."

"No you wouldn't," he said, quite patient now. "You'd sing the way you did on the cliff. No build-up and no strain. You'll just wander into the spotlight, and we'll toss it away. Don't you understand? It's that innocent beat of yours. They've never heard anything like it. Nobody has." His fingers drummed a fast rhythm on her wrist. "You've got to trust me. You've got to believe I know this racket. I ought to. I've been digging the jazz circuits since I was fourteen. I've heard 'em sing good, and I've heard 'em cut their own throats, but I've heard only a few who could even touch you when they started. Anyway, you're among friends here. Just a social evening. What have you got to lose?"

Laura was beginning to wish she could work up

some enthusiasm for the idea, because then it wouldn't seem so improbable. It was just barely possible too, with Burny's genius to support her, that she might get through a public performance without making too big a fool of herself.

Uncertainty was pulling her in two. She said "But what'll Gil think? Two rehearsals and I'm in the act! What happens when he shows up and finds me learning on his piano?"

"He can play it or go chew his fingernails," Burny said. "I'll admit I owe him a lot, but I don't ever remember electing him to do my thinking for me."

"You're being unfair, Burny. You know that," she said after a moment. "And Gil's your partner. Don't you think you ought to consider his opinion at least?"

"He was my partner back in Chicago, but nobody considered nobody."

She stared down at her hands for a dozen silent moments. Then she spread them flat on the table, to brace herself. "All right," she said. "But I'm not dressed for a debut. I'm still wearing the same old blouse and skirt I started out with this morning, and they're as wrinkled as I am."

"O.K., O.K.," Burny said, waving her off with irritation. "Go home and change. But keep it simple. No production, see? That's the whole idea tonight. And do me one favor. If you run into Gil, don't ask him about this—*tell* him."

Talisman Lake had blued to a gleam of metal in the dusk. On the chance that Gil might have stalled somewhere between Spider Island and the far cluster of lights that located Conover's Store, Laura took the grand tour before turning north to the point. Nothing was on the lake, not even sail.

The woods were a dark froth of shadow behind her lighted cabin. The silence was heavy, but she could hear a faint and sultry beat coming from her hi-fi.

She felt her footsteps falter before they stopped her on the reed-edged path. Through the open window she saw Gil first. Then she saw her sister.

She saw the golden gleam of Jan's shoulders as she drifted up to Gil and lighted his cigarette. Jan was laughing, and they both carried drinks that needed refilling.

They didn't seem particularly surprised when Laura opened the door. They looked as if they had patched up whatever difficulties had kept them apart.

Chapter Twelve

With her eyes gleaming, Jan said, "Well, don't just stand there, Laura. You warned me that Gil might show up here. When he did, I invited him in."

"It was a big, beautiful reunion," Gil put in. "With a surprise in every drink." As if to prove it, he gripped his glass and lifted it to Laura in a gesture of pure disillusion. "Anyway, cheers. *Sister*," he said, and drained off the last shallow inch like a man taking bitter medicine for the good of his soul.

The liquor itself hadn't phased him, Laura realized. She watched him set down the empty glass. It was only then that she managed to hold his gaze, so dark and cold that he must have moved long ago from the initial shock of finding Jan hiding here in her own cabin to a staling and embittered indifference.

"Gil, I'm sorry," she said above the muted throb of the music. "I knew you'd run into Jan sooner or later and discover we were sisters, and when you did, I wasn't going to lie about it. But I couldn't tell you. I'd promised her not to. Anyway, after last night—well, you said it didn't matter so much. Finding her, I mean."

"Some fine points in logic," Gil said. "Remind me to split them with you sometime."

"Yes, and don't sound so noble about it," Jan said to her as she dropped onto the couch and stretched her legs across the clutter of magazines on the coffee table.

Nuzzling Phut-Phat against the shoulder of her black satin dress, Jan went on coldly. "You didn't tell him I was here because I didn't want you telling anyone. I was scared of Harry, and I still am! Do we have to go through it all over again? Gil knows the score now."

"Well, you've explained why you never came near Burny after he was hurt," Gil told Jan.

"I couldn't. I told you that!" Jan shouted at him. "I didn't know what else Harry might do. I was afraid he might try to have you beaten up again. Or me! But I ran away from him in Miami, didn't I? Doesn't that count for anything?"

"Sure. For not having brains enough to see through a jealous brute like that in the first place. I'd give a lot to see him," Gil said, his voice knotting. "I'd give a lot to meet him. Just once. In private! What is it with him, anyway? Charm?"

Jan shot him a perplexed look, then shrugged. "Money, at first. The dizzy thought of being married to it! And I was crazy about him for a while. Anyway, you know me. And I never pretended to be any different that I am, did I? Anyway," she aid, turning to toss the words at her sister, "Gil's not as mad as he looks. We've had a nice long afternoon and I've explained the whole thing."

"All of it?" Laura asked her in a level tone.

"All of it." Jan's voice was flat, but her eyes begged for that last inch of pride while Gil was listening, and Laura understood that Jan had not told Gil about the four thousand dollars she had "taken accidentally."

Laura's eyes went to Gil just as Gil's cold stare slid away from her and happened to catch on the edge of his watch. The change in his expression was almost ludicrous.

"Good Lord! *Burny*," Gil muttered on a note of self-castigation. "Do you know where he is? I left him parked in your boat early this afternoon."

"So I discovered. Burny's all right. He's waiting in the Tavern Room, Laura said.

"So I'm late," Gil snapped. "Is he sore about it?"

"Not exactly. We spent the afternoon together turning me into a polished professional, and now I'm supposed to go back and prove it. Frankly, Gil, he doesn't care very much if you show up or not."

"For what?" Jan asked blankly.

"For my debut. I'm supposed to sing. Tonight I'm supposed to prove that I'm Burny's answer to jazz."

"You're kidding!" Jan said, putting her feet on the floor. "You only met him two days ago."

130

But Jan's hoot wasn't as hard to bear as Gil's silence. He had pushed his hands hard into his pockets.

Laura said to him, "You don't think I can do it, do you?"

"You may. If you don't push and keep it simple," he said. "The Tavern Room isn't Birdland on a Saturday night. You'll be among friends, won't you?"

"That's what Burny said."

She waited, her eyes begging him to tell her not to do it—or that he didn't want her to do it.

He said, "If Burny says you're ready, you're ready. I never argue with genius."

"No. You just meddle from the sidelines!" Laura said hotly. "Well, I tried to warn you, Gil. If you're not careful, you may wind up without a partner."

"Why don't we go find out?" he suggested with more control than she had.

"I'll need ten minutes to change," Laura said.

"Take fifteen. Burny can keep 'em listening without either of us."

When she re-entered the room where Jan was juggling the kitten, one of Gil's dark eyebrows lifted slightly, but the rest of his face remained still. He made no comment on the white cotton sheath dress, the high heels, the way she had brushed her black hair loose around her shoulders. He just jerked at the doorknob and said, "We'd better cut out."

131

"Wait a minute. What about me?" Jan demanded, stopping them both.

Her gaze flicked nervously from Laura to Gil and then back to her sister again. The kitten was struggling to get free, but Jan seemed unaware of it. She hung onto the tiny thing with a trembling hand.

"What about you?" Laura asked her with the tired patience of defeat.

"I don't want to stay here alone any more. Not for hours and hours. You think that's so pleasant?"

"Then come with us," said Laura.

"I can't. You know I can't!"

"Then I'll leave you my boat, and we'll go in Gil's. You could take a spin—"

"I don't want to be *alone*," Jan shrilled.

"Take it easy, Jan," Gil said with his back to the night. "I think you've got this Harry on the brain. I doubt if you're as important to him as you think."

"Someone tried to get in here this afternoon," Jan cried. "Or some*thing*. That's what brought Gil in off the lake—because I started screaming."

"And there was nothing," Gil said. "You know that. I searched around for half an hour." He turned his head and looked at the sister in white. "I thought it was you screaming," he said evenly. "I thought maybe you were entertaining your polished friend with the dogs. I didn't want to interfere, but it sounded as if things were getting out of hand."

When they were outside her cabin, Laura said tensely, "Gil—do you think she's in any real danger from this man?"

"I don't know. I think he's warped, jealous, and ugly. He may even be a mental case. If all she did was jilt him in Miami—but she may not be telling the truth. It doesn't exactly run in the family, does it?"

"Oh, Gil—Gil, I couldn't tell you that Jan and I were sisters. She came home frightened to death of being seen by anyone. She seemed half sick and desperate. I hadn't even heard from her in three years. I wanted to help her if I could—but it was such a miserable problem. I thought perhaps she'd decide to go away again if I just kept quiet and let her rest here awhile. Gil, can't you understand?"

"I'm trying to, he said. "But I started telling you about Jan and Burny and me the first half-hour we met, and you listened. You kept those quiet beautiful eyes on me, and all the time you knew who Jan Talis was and where she was. I don't know which rocked me worse—bursting into your cabin like a damned fool and finding her there, or realizing you could lie as well as she ever could."

"I've never lied to you!"

"All right. You didn't lie. You just took the negative approach. But let's go, shall we? Burny's waiting."

She watched him turn away from her and stride down the path, a figure as lonely as he was stubborn. He left her to follow him as best she could past the black shape of her outboard. Her high heels tripped her once on the wooden slats of the pier, and her legs were trembling as she climbed into Gil's borrowed boat.

She watched him cast off and then settle himself behind the wheel. The waves that rocked them gently only deepened the ache of her distress. She smoothed the white dress over her knees, then locked her hands together.

She said, "You have a way of twisting everything, Gil. Even that remark you made about my entertaining Mr. Lasher— You knew I was with Burny all afternoon. You made sure of that yourself!"

"I made sure of nothing," Gil said as he turned his set profile away and backed them into deep water. "All I did was leave Burny waiting in your boat this noon, and that was strictly his own idea. I tried to talk him out of it. I didn't know when you'd show up, and I couldn't very well tell him where you were."

"I don't see why not."

"He still thinks you're uncomplicated."

"Gil, you're impossible! When I returned Mr. Lasher's cigarette case, he gave me a perfectly good explanation for losing it and then he invited me to stay for lunch. That's all!"

"*All*," Gil echoed. "You must have been in his bungalow for hours. I found out that much when I checked with Samuels about you."

134

"Would it be simpler if I punched a time card for you?"

"Well, what was I supposed to do? I was worried about Burny. I didn't want to leave him parked there alone in your boat, and I didn't know how to tell him where you were. So I decided to double back from Conover's Store as soon as I got our supplies and try to persuade him to come back to the island with me. Only, when I was passing the point, I heard a girl screaming. I thought it was you and Lasher. Who else?"

For a moment there was only the sound of the white water hissing away from the prow, and then Gil added, "I wish I'd let things alone. I must have looked like the biggest fool on earth, bursting in there."

"You'd have found out about Jan and me sooner or later," Laura mumbled.

"I suppose so. I just wish you'd told me yourself. Or let me find it out a little easier."

He was setting a straight course for Lee's Landing across the starlit expanse of water. She felt the warm breeze of night on her lips, but suddenly it had a different taste. The first subtle trace of autumn, remembered from many earlier summers. Soon the black bulk of Spider Island would flame up briefly like a torch of farewell for summer's end.

There had been several years when she had roughed it alone at the lake until the first snow sealed the landscape. That had been fun. She had been alone, but not lonely. She had never felt a trapped and futile loneliness until this moment.

She said, "It's funny, but we don't seem to have any existence of our own. We just revolve around other people. We take on their problems and try to be responsible for their faults. You and I have never had five minutes for just *us*. Do you realize we've never had an ordinary conversation, Gil, or even laughed over a joke? I'm not sure we've even seen each other or heard each other. I think we're just shadows cast by other people. We're too weak to be anything else." She laughed hollowly. "I keep wondering what it would have been like if we'd met on the island and had it all ordinary and simple."

"It would have been wonderful," Gil said.

"Do you mean that?"

"Why do you think I keep wanting to take you in my arms?"

"I don't know," she said miserably. "Those two times—I thought maybe it was just because I wanted you to. But that doesn't help, either. We still never get around to saying anything that matters. About us, I mean."

"Oh, Laura—" He moved restlessly like a man about to stifle a groan. He reached for her hand and began to rub it hard against his jaw.

"Aren't we going to have any chance at all?" she asked him in a small voice.

"Where do we start? Who do we pretend doesn't exist? Burny? Your own sister? Now even this guy Lasher seems to want in. What's the use?" Gil sighed and released her hand. "That's been the trouble all along—how to get out from under other people."

"I don't think you've tried very hard—the way you've pushed me at Burny from the very beginning."

"It wouldn't have made much difference if I hadn't. You happen to have a voice, and Burny caught it. He would have sooner or later. Nobody could change that angle."

"I'm not so sure. I may be a flop tonight," she said, grinning weakly.

"I wouldn't bet on it."

"Then I could try to flop. Deliberately."

"Why hurt him like that?" Gil said, staring ahead. "Hasn't he had enough already?"

They flew in darkness, the spray hissing, the lighted terrace ahead of them and great shining windows of the Lodge spreading a golden net across the waters.

She drew a broken breath. "Gil—"

But already he had sealed up that small channel of communication that had opened between them.

She began to feel a creeping dullness. She said, "Are you going to tell him about Jan, or shall I?"

"Just so somebody does," Gil said as they jarred into the dock. "A little truth might clear the air for all of us."

Chapter Thirteen

Afterward, in order to block out the desperation and the tragedy of that night, Laura always tried to think of it as simply "the night she sang with Burny."

Had she, she wondered, actually enjoyed that brief and electric experience in the spotlight? Something, at least, had helped get her through it, although it hadn't been Gil's support, musically or otherwise.

From the moment the two of them had walked into the Tavern Room and found Burny perched like a castaway on his stool, already captivating the crowded room, Gil had seemed to deliver her up to the blind guitarist.

It was Burny who tossed off the casual announcement: "This girl most of you know already. Personally, I think she ought to give up swimming for jazz." It was Burny who led her into the easy lilt of "It Had To Be You," and it was Burny who whispered, "O.K., chick. It's all yours."

Gil was there, hunched over his little piano at the edge of the spotlight, his hands thumping out an accompaniment dull enough to bewilder anyone. But after the second group of songs, there were periods when Gil just didn't play at all— when he'd seem to dissolve into the murmurous background of the Tavern Room where the bar floated like a raft in the sea-green gloom and where other shadows whispered and smoked, making soft noises with their glasses and sometimes breaking into applause. And into even sharper applause whenever she and Burny shared the spotlight alone.

Was that because she and Burny—without a piano; at least, without a piano played so poorly— made a novel pair? Or a "new sound?" Singing in such a trance of nerves and unreality, Laura wasn't sure of anything.

The whole experience was strange and informal and treacherously exciting. The faceless people who clapped really seemed to like her. They were even willing to forgive her more than one bad moment of clumsiness, laughing with her and demanding more.

"What do you mean *why?*" Burny muttered, grinning as they wrapped up another group of the blues. "It's that lost-angel style of yours. You've got 'em way out tonight!"

But even Burny's excitement couldn't warm up Laura's inner chill of disbelief. This was happening to someone else. Not to Laura Brown.

Perhaps that was why she reacted so stupidly when Mr. Samuels bustled up between numbers to give her his managerial blessing.

"Well, I must say, Laura! Why didn't you let me in on this? I'd have gotten out some advance publicity. Hiding a talent like this—it's unbelievable! Quite a bit of excitement for everyone tonight. I wish you could hear the talk. Even Mr. Lasher's been asking questions. I think he's making plans for you already."

"But that's ridiculous. This is just a —a kind of crazy prank tonight."

But it wasn't, of course. By the time Burny was ready to release her with a murmured command— "You'd better wrap it up after the next chorus. No need to give 'em as much as they want"—she realized that what had happened had its own meaning, as undeniable as the triumph that flowed from Burny like some hidden radiation.

Marred by the black glasses, his bony face seemed as bloodless and shining as a statue's, the mouth curved and cold with pleasure. And something else—the way he held his head, freer, moving it with an ease she'd never seen before.

Was he able to see tonight? she wondered. Sometimes vision seemed concentrated on her like a secret beam.

Several times she tried to communicate a look of questioning to Gil, but he might have been blind himself. His face was as tired as Burny's was transfixed. Had Gil noticed nothing, then? One thing, he couldn't help but be aware of how uniquely her voice and Burny's guitar blended together. Without him.

140

Together, she and Burny spun out the last lingering phrase of "Wanting You." Across the burst of applause, Burny said, "We'd better take ten ourselves. Gil sounds like he's playing on an empty cigarbox."

But Gil cramped sidewise under the toy piano, didn't even unwind his legs.

"Gil—?" Laura whispered.

"Run along," he said. "You've got a public now. People want to congratulate you."

"And you don't?" she asked.

"I just want things to work out for you and Burny," Gil said. "That might make up for some of the mistakes I've made."

"Gil—*please*—I've got to talk to you."

"Sure. Any time." His big shoulders moved with a sudden restlessness. "But you'd better run along now. And smile, honey. People are looking at you. This is your night."

She wasn't sure how she escaped to the powder room, but she had pushed impatiently past people who wanted to detain her.

And Harrison Lasher had been one of them, but standing apart from them, she remembered as the heavy door to the powder room billowed shut behind her. And he was wearing gray again.

But what had he said? She remembered the tone of his voice clearly enough—as much in command as if he had been talking to his dogs—but the actual words eluded her. Something about a little celebration for her after the Tavern Room had closed

141

—some long-distance calls he'd already put through—the head of a recording company in Chicago—a top-flight band leader—anything she wanted—

She had begun to lose him completely there.

"But you don't understand, Mr. Lasher—"

"Harrison. I think it's time you loosened up a littel with me," he had said, smiling.

"Harrison." In her confusion, she had even repeated it after him. "But I'm not a singer. Tonight just happened!"

"Now, now. You're just excited. We'll decide all this later."

"There's nothing to decide," she had mumbled.

"I'm going to help you. Besides—after that luncheon by the pool—I thought we were friends."

"We are."

"A girl with your beauty, Laura—did you really think I'd let you stay buried here? There were a number of possibilities. This makes it simpler for both of us."

In the multiple mirrors of the powder room that were as empty and soft-tinted as a sigh, Laura watched a dozen girls draw paper cups and fill them at the water coolers. Then two women came in and stopped dead at the sight of her.

"Oh, Miss Brown!" one of them said, giggling. "We thought you were simply wonderful. And your very first appearance, too—I mean, it's like an event!"

They even demanded her unsteady autograph on two matchbooks.

She managed to reach the fresh air of the terrace without further encounters, but she felt soured by their silliness. Grown women. And only yesterday she had been teaching their children how to float.

Three busboys and the headwaiter from the Lodge's dining room were crossing the terrace with a pair of folding buffet tables, a load of silver and linen, and two champagne buckets. Behind them, a barboy pushed a loaded liquor cart. They helped each other negotiate the stops, and then they took the white-raked path that let toward Bungalow 10.

So Harrison Lasher's "little celebration" for her wasn't to be a private one. She felt relief, followed by a sense of helplessness. She didn't have to go, of course. But then he hadn't actually forced her to remain alone with him for hours that afternoon by his glittering pool behind the wall.

For a moment she rested her elbows heavily on the stone parapet and closed her eyes. When she opened them, she was looking across the water at Spider Island. That lovely, harsh sunctuary from the woes of childhood! What a sweet relief it would be just to run down to the dock's end, to slide into the watery silence, and, with long strokes, to strike out for the far free shores.

The phantasy was so strong, she even felt the muscles tighten in her legs and shoulders. And then the impulse itself flickered out because Burny was beside her.

Had he moved straight across the terrace or been forced to feel his way along the curved wall? Her glance darted to the doorway, where Gil still stood, and then anger stiffened her. Having safely delivered his friend, what was he waiting for?

She watched Gil hold up five fingers—probably meaning five minutes—and then she saw him frown and warningly shake his head at her.

Well, that was plain too. He meant, *Forget what I said. Don't tell him about Jan just yet. Don't spoil tonight for him.*

And Burny was grasping her hand as he said, "Laura, you were wonderful! Wasn't I right? Didn't I tell you? We've got it made!"

His upper lip was damp, and the reflection on his glasses danced like lightning across a barrier of heat. He was in a state, and the state was contagious.

Her face lifted as he pulled her against him, and their mingling laughter was more vibration than sound. She said, "Burny—will you listen to me for just a minute? I mean, really listen?"

"Sure. But none of that jazz about quitting. You're just bushed. The world looks black. You want to know something? That up-and-down reaction is chronic with real talent." He locked his fingers behind her back and rocked her. "I'll tell

144

you something else. I could *feel* that crowd watching you and wanting more. And then all at once I saw your face."

They stood stock-still. Her hand went to her throat, and her heart began to pound.

"I wasn't going to tell you yet," Burny said. "It came, and then it went. Like a fuse blowing out on a vision. Then everything blurred. But you're dark, aren't you? And you're beautiful," he whispered. "The way Gil said you were."

She said something thickly—his name twice—before she was able to say, "Oh, Burny, we've got to find Gil! We've got to tell him—"

"Not yet. Not till I'm sure."

"But even this much—it will mean everything to Gil. Burny, you just don't realize—"

"I said *no*," Burny said. "I don't want him fussing at me or yapping for a doctor. When the time comes, I don't want to need anyone's help. I want to be able to look him in the face and not have to ask for one more favor."

"Burny, you're wrong," she whispered. "Gil understands more than you think."

"I love him, too," Burny told her. "You think I'm kidding? I owe Gil more than I can ever repay. But I want free of him when the time comes. Is that so wrong?"

"No. But you've both been under a terrible strain, Burny. You could lift it a little for Gil if you'd only—"

"The only strain I've been under is wanting to see you," the guitarist said.

When Burny kissed her, she felt the heat of her own tears and then a sudden urge to let the moment break and incandesce. Even when his kiss deepened on her lips, she felt herself respond.

Yet she had known that Gil was standing in the doorway again, watching them, waiting to guide Burny back to the Tavern Room. Had she let it happen or made it happen? She wondered.

She even drifted up to Gil with Burny's fingers still linking her own. And then she felt like a sleepwalker putting a cold foot on a gritty floor and awakening to reality. Surely she wasn't going to have to explain that that kiss had been born of impulse and defiance.

Her eyes must have pleaded with Gil, but he didn't avoid them. There was a shadow, both tired and impersonal, on his face.

Gil said to Burny, "You ordered a ten-minute break, kid. It's over twenty."

"O.K. Let's wrap it up. Then we'll help her celebrate."

"Not me," Gil said quietly. "I'll wait it out for you somewhere and pick you up afterwards."

"But this is a party for Laura. Didn't Samuels brief you? Some resorter named Lasher is setting up free champagne and caviar for everyone. He's supposed to have some big connections. He might even do us some good. The least we can do is provide a little dance music."

"Then you provide it," Gil told him. "They'll settle for you, Burny. Besides, I met a girl this afternoon. I think maybe I'll look her up again."

"Since the celebration's for Laura, I still think you ought to show," Burny repeated peevishly.

"I don't like the man who's putting it on," Gil said.

"Lasher? I thought he was a friend of Laura's."

"He is, and he's very nice," she said.

"Then what's the beef?" Burny demanded.

"He keeps too many dogs," Gil said.

Burny shrugged and then muttered, "Suit yourself. But watch it for the last half, will you? I never heard you play such a bad piano."

"I doubt if anyone even noticed it," Gil replied.

As she followed the two of them toward the Tavern Room, Laura tried desperately to get Gil's attention.

"Gil—?" she whispered.

"We're late already," he said as he shouldered open the heavy door for his frined.

"But just for a minute. Please," she said.

"Can't you give her a minute?" Burny snapped at him. "From here I can find my own way."

So they were left alone in a lobby dotted with people, standing in the fitful breeze from the driftwood door.

"Gil, do I have to explain?" she said.

"I haven't asked you to."

"But you're angry. You're hurt." She drew a

breath. "What you saw out there didn't mean a thing."

"It's all right if it did. Can't you understand something? I *want* things to work out for you and Burny. Success—happiness—anything good you can salvage."

"Gil, I could flay you. You'll never say anything important about us, will you? Or make it easy for me to say it!"

"I thought we'd said most of it out on the lake tonight," Gil answered.

"About *us*? Or the way we let other people come first? I like Burny and I love his talent, but he isn't the world to me, and I'm tired of feeling guilty because I can't feel sorry for him every minute. He's had some bad breaks, but so have you. So have I and so has Jan! I kissed Burny because we were both excited and because I wanted to, I guess. But mostly because he's beginning to see again."

Gil said something like "What—?"

She said, "He saw my face tonight—clearly, I guess—but he doesn't want you to know. He's afraid it won't last, and he doesn't want you to start mothering him again. But he's not blind any more, Gil. I don't know—I think he's afraid to admit to himself how much he really can see."

She watched Gil brush his hand across his face.

"Thank God," he breathed. "That's all I ever wanted—prayed somebody could do for him. *You.* Somehow I knew it would be you—" He had to pause. "I'll leave him alone. I'll cut out of here tonight—for good—if that'll make it easier for him."

She stood still and made him look at her until his eyes were almost black and he said, "Laura—Laura—I *can't* tell him how I feel about you."

"Have you told yourself?"

"I live with it! Your precious voice doesn't mean a thing to me, and neither does your relationship with Jan. I meddled—I pushed you at Burny—but something good's come out of that, at least. If it were just you and me—if I could carry you off to that island of yours and spend the rest of our lives beachcombing, I'd die a happy man."

"But you can't tell that to Burny."

"I can't do the same thing to him twice," Gil said, his face pale.

"Burny's tougher than you think," she murmured. "And he's selfish—did you know that? He might even bear up under the shock of losing me."

"And he might go blind again and stay that way. Laura, I'm to blame for what happened to that guy. *Me!* If I can't live with you, I've still got to live with myself."

"You know what I think?" she said. "I think Burny will be playing his guitar long after Rome's burned down for both of us."

They had to move apart then because the two women who had demanded her autograph went sailing past them into the Tavern Room, elbowing each other at the sight of her and tittering. Laura

149

flashed them a neon smile, then let herself sag again.

Gil stood fiddling with the change in his pockets. He didn't seem to know how to leave her. And she had to make one final try.

"Gil, I won't stay at the party. I'll make some excuse—"

"No, I think I'll look up Jan—"

"Jan?" she said.

"I've been thinking about her a lot. I think she really tried to level with me. And she's in a state. Maybe I can persuade her to clear out of here."

"She won't go," Laura whispered. "She won't even listen."

"She may listen to me."

"For old time's sake?"

"You don't forget a girl like Jan," Gil told her. "You don't forget war and earthquake, either. But the way I see it, we're both expendable. You and Burny would be better off if neither one of us were around."

Chapter Fourteen

Against the background of the pressing woods, Bungalow 10 was lighted up with a festive brilliance.

Even the front door stood open, proclaiming "open house" to any guest at Lee's Landing who wanted to help celebrate the debut of a home-grown talent—one Laura Brown, ex-swimming teacher, tonight's new promise for the nation's jukeboxes.

Well, I tried and I'm not trying any more. I've had it, Laura thought, vaguely conscious that she was dragging her feet beside Burny's on the gravel walk, uncertain just who was leading whom to Harrison Lasher's party. Gil wasn't going to reject his principles. Instead, from the most decent and honest motives, he had rejected her.

"Laura—?" came Burny's voice beside her.

"What?"

"Come on, come on! Get through to me, doll. I've asked you three times if you thought this Lasher might do us some good? Samuels said he's a big wheel. Plenty of influence and connections—even in the music world."

"I don't know. He mentioned something like that. I—I'm not sure now what he said."

It took an effort to force Bungalow 10 back into perspective—to see its open door framing lights, people—a man in gray with a pink drink in his hand.

"He's really throwing a ball for you," Burny said with that note of intensity that had driven him all evening.

"Burny—you mean you can really see all this?" she exclaimed.

"I can hear it. Yeah, I guess I can see it, too. That's a patio wall, isn't it—casting a green shadow along the top. You don't suppose he stacks his money in there, do you?"

"Huh-uh. Not big enough. This is a very chi-chi bungalow. Behind that wall is a private pool complete with watchdogs."

"Can't he swim in the lake?"

"He can't swim, period." And with a laugh, "Oh, Burny—Burny, I'm so happy for you tonight!"

"So am I. But, Lord. Stick close to me, will you?" he said, gripping her hand. "I feel like I'm walking on a live wire. Everything's too bright. One slip and the fuse may blow again."

That, Laura realized, was probably why he refused to remove the black glasses—he was still unwilling to trust himself. She wondered suddenly if a shock could topple him back into blindness. That had been the very danger Gil had feared, using it as an excuse to protect Burny and to walk away from love.

Well, Gil needn't worry any more, she told herself. It was better to be needed than rejected. Better to share a joy ride to success with a genius like Burny than to nurse a cold crust of heart-break alone.

With smiling eyes and tilted head, she sailed into Bungalow 10 with a fine and careless bravado.

A goup of jazz enthusiasts soon had Burny enshrined in a corner, where he began to play South American rhythms with a beat as complex as it was unnerving. Someone presently added a pair of bongos. Couples began to dance beside the pool. Clutching another of those terrible persimmon drinks that Mr. Lasher's houseboy had borne aloft to her on an individual tray shining like a platinum coin, Laura circulated among the well-heeled guests of Lee's Landing who only yesterday would have thought she was pushing herself in company like this.

"—but it's quite fabulous, my dear. I mean here you've been teaching Junior how to swim all summer and now this!"

"—a little like Peggy Lee, then?"

"Not at all. But there's a quality—reminds me of that singer who's made such a hit with those West Coast jazz groups."

"Ridiculous. I tell you this girl's unique. She

needs plenty of work, but she has a very cool charge. I predict in a year—"

Laura began to wonder if something was wrong with the air-conditioning unit. Her face felt hot and her brains heavy. Cigarette smoke veiled the chattering faces, and shafts of conversation drifted past her with increasing vagueness. How long was it since she had slept the sleep of wonderful unconsciousness? She kept mentally slipping off, treading time, wrestling with the stresses of uncertainty. And now and then she found herself glancing nervously under a chair or into a corner, but those crazy dogs weren't here either.

She thought again of Spider Island, and of the haven it had been when she was a child. Then she remembered Jan—and Gil. Gil was with her sister—

On a chipped laugh, Laura went into the arms of her host.

"Beginning to enjoy yourself?" he asked her.

"It's marvelous!"

"I'm glad you've decided to be reasonable," Harrison Lasher said.

Even the expensively scented lotion he must have misted across his well-shaven jaw had a steely essence, she thought, and he danced the way she had known he would—expertly. In comparison, she began to feel as if she were doing the samba on someone else's tangling legs.

"Perhaps you're tired," he suggested after her third fiasco.

"I must be! I can't seem to follow you at all."

"Well, you're new at it," he said with an oblique laugh. "And I do have my little peculiarities. However, you'll learn. As soon as we leave here, I've promised myself the pleasure of educating you in a number of things."

"Leave?"

"Tomorrow. Didn't I tell you?"

"Mr. Lasher—"

"Harrison."

He had her arm, and for some reason she was allowing him to walk her toward a small gate in the wall. With the green light of the pool behind them, they cast a green shadow that kept growing longer and more distorted.

"I'm not going anywhere," she said.

"I just want to call my babies. I'm afraid I shouldn't have let them run loose for so long tonight."

"I didn't mean that," she said as he drew her through the gate onto a dark path, his heavy ring pressed deep against her arm.

She watched him put two fingers to his lips and give a low whistle. He said mildly, "They're really very good and obedient. But then they know what happens when they're not."

Again he put his fingers to his mouth and whistled for his dogs. "I should have brought them in sooner. But a little hunt on their own always sharpens them. Would you like to walk a bit?"

"Not particularly."

"You seem pale. A little air will do you good."

Free to turn away, she began to move beside him. Out here, only a greenish shadow of light disfigured the treetops, and Burny's guitar reached her like a faint-threaded plaint.

"Ah-h! Here they come," Harrison Lasher murmured happily.

The pair of animals burst into the clearing with such a low and beastly yelping that she was shaken.

"They're not even safe to be loose!" she told him. "You know one of them killed something near my own cabin."

"Djong. It's bred in the blood back to Australian bush days. Cigarette?"

She shook her head.

"I keep forgetting how rare you are," he said. "Beauty without even the smaller vices."

She heard his platinum cigarette case snap shut, followed by the rasping flare of a lighter that gleamed on his ring. One of the dogs was still running around through the grass. She felt the other one stalk her carefully, then sniff her feet.

It was now or never, and she spoke much too loudly. "I'd really like to know what you meant when we were dancing. I'm not going anywhere tomorrow."

"You're leaving with me for Chicago," he said. "Everything's been arranged. Auditions, bookings —even a shopping tour."

"And just like that. No tiresome details, I suppose, and without even bothering to ask me or to consult Burny."

"From the way you were acting tonight, I thought you'd decided to be reasonable," he said.

"I thought so too. 'Laura', I said to myself, 'be reasonable. Everyone wants you to sing, so sing. Have yourself a career. Even Mr. Lasher wants to help you.' Only it's not that simple, of course."

"That depends. You're auditioning for Simplex Records first, then with the Cato Mendez Trio. A week from tonight, you'll be singing at my club in Miami."

"If I sing anywhere at all, it will be with Burny. And he has a contract right here till the season ends."

"That blind bum. Who needs him?"

Her hand went to her throat, but she didn't step backward. Caution flickered in her mind. Was this man insane? she wondered. His queer spells of emptiness. There were split personalities, weren't there?

"I see," she whispered.

"Do you? You're gorgeous, but apparently not so bright. Voice or no voice, I'd never have left a treasure like you behind."

Mingling with fear came an angry humiliation. She said to him, "I agree—no one could have been denser. My career! Thanks again, but no thanks, Mr. Lasher."

"If you can't say Harrison, try 'Harry,'" he suggested.

Just then a faint sound of laughter reached her. Someone must have fallen into the pool.

"Harry?" she whispered.

"Harry Lasher Warrigal. That's why I bought my first pair."

"Of what?" she asked him.

"Of dogs. I told you once—they're Australian dingoes. They're also called warrigals. I liked that —owning a breed with same name as mine. If I'd had Djong and Wallah along when your sister ran out on me in Miami, they might have changed her mind. And her face."

All along, she thought. *Little signs.* Little bits and perplexities that she should have fitted together. But Jan had exaggerated after all about Harry Warrigal wanting to kill her if he ever found her. He'd only set his dogs loose on her. It would be an accident, of course. A dreadful accident, and the dogs would have to be shot. Well, he had a kennel full of them, didn't he?

And who would blame their master? Harrison Lasher might even insist on paying the hospital bills, and Jan would come out with plastic surgery holding her together while her mind gibbered on the verge of breakdown.

"How did you know where to find her?" Laura mumbled.

"Money can always buy information. And Jan always did have a big mouth when she drank too much. I knew there was a Talisman Lake somewhere and a big sister who'd raised her. The sur-

158

prise came when I found out how beautiful the sister really was."

Numbly, Laura siad, "I'll make her give you back that money—"

His laugh slurred in the darkness. "Do you think I followed her here to get back a few measly dollars? I don't even want *her* back! But I warned her once—I told her what would happen if she ever tried to leave me. Well, she did! She ratted out on me just to pick up that jerk I tried to warn her away from once before. She walked out on me— *me*—for a piano player. He must have fixed it up. He was right here waiting for her. You think I'm going to take that? This time I'll find somebody who'll finish the job on him!"

"But he didn't even know Jan was here," Laura said on a breaking gasp. "And my sister didn't come here to meet him. It—it just happened."

He turned a look of such venom on her that she put her hands on her cheeks. She knew that he'd led her easily into what was coming and that she'd have to spring the trap herself.

"All right," she said. "All right. I'll go with you."

"Alone. And no more talk about bringing blind boy and his guitar along for accompaniment."

"I'll hardly need him, will I?"

"Just me," Harry Warrigal said, smiling. "Be reasonable, and I can put you on top."

"Will you let them alone? Both of them? Both my sister and Gil Bricker?"

"As long as you marry me and stay married to me," he said.

And his dingoes came yelping up to whimper at his ringed hand.

Chapter Fifteen

She dared not tell Gil because he might try to do something rash. She didn't know how to tell Burny yet. And telling Jan wouldn't matter one way or another.

I must look like the dead, Laura thought as she re-entered the gate in the wall on the arm of her host. With the pair of wet-tongued little dingoes padding at their heels, the two of them skirted the iridescent pool and the buffet tables and the dancing couples who looked so normal, who called out quite sanely, "Heh, you two!" And, "We thought we'd lost you." And "How about a song, Miss Brown?"

"She'd love to. Wouldn't you, Laura?" said the man in gray.

"All right."

As he turned away, she stared at his smooth shoulders and easy stride. There was no name to use for him. He belonged in a case book in a doctor's office with bars at the window.

When Burny's guitar began to whisper the deepblue chording of "Night and Day," she must have fallen in with the beat, because presently hands were clapping and when someone asked for more, she shook her head.

161

"Something wrong?" Burny asked in a quiet aside.

She said, "Everything's great."

"You mean Lasher mentioned some contacts?"

"Simplex Records. His club in Miami, too."

"Man! What'd I tell you? In six month we'll be living off the fat." Burny's bony wrist twanged a gleeful chord. "Come on, doll. Let's get this next one off the ground."

"You get it off, Burny. I'm leaving."

"But the party's great."

"So stay! I mean, you'd better stay," she amended, trying to hang onto control. "I'm too tired to run you out to the island, and anyway, Gil said he'd pick you up."

"But Laura—"

His tone of complaint only made her move away faster. His time of needing her had better be over.

Would Harrison Lasher let Jan and Gil alone? she wondered. Probably yes, she decided. As long as she was settled beside him in that gray Chrysler tomorrow—as obedient as his chained babies on the back seat—and no one suspected the truth behind her departure.

Least of all Gil! If Gil objected—if he even tried to argue with the impeccable Mr. Lasher—Gil might wind up unpleasantly dead. Not here, of course, or now. Perhaps not for a month, but somewhere.

Far across the split-level interior of Bungalow

10 stood the open door. No one stopped her from trying to reach it. Not even the starched houseboy who was bearing another tray of pink horrors toward the pool, nor the dogs, who padded beside her and then dropped on their haunches at the threshold, held no farther by a rigid obedience, their incurious attention following her as she began to run down the gravel walk toward the dark refuge of the lake.

Her high heels beat a tattoo on wood, and she wondered if she might not have run straight off the end of the dock if this man hadn't simply put out his arms and let her run into him instead.

The impact was hard enough to make him grunt. Her hands clutched at his shirt. When she saw who it was, she simply buried her face against him.

He seemed to know how to hold her until she quieted. There was nothing personal in the way he did it, just firmly and with enough patience to wait out that interval between a possible scream and a giggle.

"You ought to learn how to drink," Gil said at last.

"Man, I had only a teeny one," she said flippantly. "All chilled and beautifully bleeding."

"So you're high on the brew of acclaim. Come on. I'll take you home."

"You'd better take Burny home. Poor Burny's going to need a home."

"It won't hurt him to wait."

"That's a switch."

"Climb in," Gil ordered with a shove. "You can be nasty on the way."

"I don't want to be anything," she mumbled, sweeping hair from her face. "I just want to get lost."

When she got to the padded seat of Gil's boat, still loaded with the groceries he'd bought at Conover's that afternoon, Laura stretched out her legs and took the revved-up vibrations like a drug. Straight up were the stars.

"Can't you go any faster?" she said. "If you can't, I can!"

"Better?" Gil asked as a sharpening whine seemed to lift them off the water.

"I just want to *go*," she whispered.

And he didn't slow down at the point to put her off, but gunned the boat on, hurtling along the curve of the shore line.

"Do you want to know something?" he said at last. "You're sitting beside a fool."

"Is that supposed to be news?"

"I thought I had no right to put you first."

"Man, I'm nowhere!"

"Look. Can't you make this a little easy for me, Laura?"

"Did you ever make it easy for me?"

"O.K. I had that coming. Will you listen now?" She stirred numbly. "Gil, it just doesn't matter any more."

"It matters to me," he said. "I had an idea I

could just resign from the whole problem. I thought if I talked Jan into clearing out with me, I'd be the boy with the halo. Only I didn't go near her. I've been rodding this boat around for hours, trying to get a look at myself."

Of course, Laura thought. *Now that it was too late. Men!* She said violently, "Then you'd better get back to Burny before you run out of gas."

"The devil with Burny!" He sucked in a breath. "I didn't mean that. It's me. With all that loyalty, I don't know how you stood me. You tried to tell me, too—I wasn't doing Burny any good. The doctors said to let him stand on his own feet, but I felt too guilty to listen. Then I tried to make you hold him up. How can a guy be so wrong? Even the dictionary puts 'love' before 'loyalty.' I don't want to hurt him. I'll try to break it easy. I think we should even stick with him for a while if that'd help—but for once I'm going to tell him what *we* want."

"I don't even remember what that was," Laura whispered.

"Just each other and the nerve to admit it out loud. Me, I mean. You knew what this was costing the three of us from the start."

She spoke with the callousness of the numb and suffering. "I wish you'd managed to say all that a little sooner, Gil. Now I want something else. I'm going to Chicago with Harrison Lasher tomorrow. Anything I want, he says, and after what happened in the Tavern Room, why shouldn't I want

165

a lot? I'm sick of being nobody at the end of no-where. Only, Burny's not included."

"Included in what?" Gil asked in a strange voice.

"In my career. Sounds funny, doesn't it? Laura Brown—from Bop to Blues! I can just go faster on my own, that's all."

"How did Burny take that news?"

"I haven't told him yet. I didn't know how to. I was hoping you'd break it to him after I was gone."

Gil looked at her intently. "No one can change that fast."

"Didn't you?"

"Not underneath. Not the way I felt about you. You *knew* that. I'm not excusing myself but—This is some kind of a gag, isn't it?"

"We're leaving tomorrow."

"You and Lasher."

"You don't have to say it like that!"

"But the guy's wrong. He's mental. Can't you feel that! Or doesn't it matter? He gets through to you, doesn't he? He did from the start."

"At least I get through to him, and he has the kind of money and influence that can make things happen. He's already arranged some top auditions and bookings for me, and I want a chance at them."

"I thought you wanted a chance for us."

"I did!" But her throat closed, saving her. She made herself shrug it off. "Then I began to think,

What's the use with you? You admitted yourself that you tried to walk out on me tonight and go back to Jan."

"I thought I was trying to admit I'd fallen in love with you. You let me say it, too. Why? For the kicks?"

"Don't—Gil—please—" she said thickly.

"Don't worry. I'm getting the message," he said as they rocketed past the island again. "We had something going, but it couldn't get off the ground."

"And you're shocked. That's very funny! If you hadn't kept pushing me at Burny, none of this would have happened. I'd probably never have gotten near enough to a spotlight to care whether I had a voice or not."

"So I was wrong. Haven't I admitted it! But Burny's caught in the middle again, and he doesn't deserve it. He thinks he discovered you, but you want to ditch him without even a thank you. Why don't you use another pair of brass knuckles on him? It would be kinder."

"Harrison Lasher says I can go faster on my own."

"I don't doubt it," Gil said. "But you can break it to Burny easy, can't you? You can give him a few days to get used to the idea."

"Still trying to protect him?"

"I don't think so. But then I wouldn't kick a blind dog without some warning, either."

"Burny isn't blind! You should have seen him at the party. He just isn't sure of himself yet."

"Well, this ought to give him quite a sense of security," Gil said. And then he laughed. "It's enough to bug you," he said. "Full circle. The only thing different is the sister."

"I was wondering when you'd start to compare us."

"I should have sooner. I even did for a while this afternoon when I found out you could lie and cover up—"

"That was different. You know it was different!"

"And you had your reasons, and I wanted to believe you were nothing like her. But the pattern was there. Sisters!"

And the dark sister said, "I think you'd better take me in."

"Why not? We've covered about everything, I'd say."

Had they? If so, why didn't he just let her stumble onto the pier without turning her face and holding it between his hands? That bitter and yet tender kiss—murmurless and unexplained—as brief a farewell as the lift of his hand as he backed into deep water.

Her gaze tried to follow the gleaming little craft, but it vanished like an arrow loosed into darkness. The wake fanned out in a foaming stain, waves lapped the piling, the water quieted.

Her eyes felt so wide and dry, they burned. Perhaps that was why she moved like a sleepwalker from the pier's end onto shore before she realized that her own red outboard was gone!

With an effort, she tried to force her beaten brain to backtrack. She stared at the iron ring where she herself had tied the boat when she had returned to the cabin and found Gil and Jan together.

Laura spun around—and as she put out her foot shock ran through her. She drew her foot back. Something small and furred lay in the broken reeds by the path—the kitten, the tiny Siamese Phut-Phat. And this time, dead.

She stepped across a wet, dark stain. There was a slashed piece of satin on the path itself. Black satin, and bloodied.

Her mind pictured Jan's golden skin beneath a horribly torn black satin dress, and the mutilated face that had been so lovely. And the dogs—the dogs of Harry Warrigal . . .

Chapter Sixteen

Laura made herself fight down the first clutch of panic. Gil was long out of earshot, so there was no use calling for help, and the impulse to run blindly had to be stifled. Whatever had happned, her sister couldn't be helped—or even found—unless she kept from going to pieces herself.

The door of her cabin stood open on a room as empty as its shadows. The orange lamp burned in its own gloom, and the twang of a blued guitar came from the hi-fi. How long, Laura wondered, had that recording been repeating itself, unattended, unheard?

The note lay on the coffee table, it's edge under an overflowing ash tray. The words had been written in an unformed and jerky scrawl.

It's hours since the Tavern Room closed. You promised to come right back, but where are you? I've got the place locked, but it's trying to get in again. I can't take this much longer—I know Harry's found me! This is just the kind of thing he'd do—try to make me crazy with fear. Sis, I'm so scared. And sorry for things. I want to be like you. I want to return the money if there's any way. There's that noise again! If it stops, I'm going to make a run for the island. You've got to help me, Laura! There's no one but you left to help me.

Indecision wavered through Laura like nausea. The island? There would be her own fatigue to battle, plus the threat of nervous exhaustion. She hadn't swum that distance in years. Yet it took her less than minutes to step out of her clothes, don a bathing suit, and reach the end of the pier again.

The lake was calm beneath the waning moon, and the water itself felt light and cool. As she lengthened out in a swimming style measured for endurance, Laura found that her thoughts were lengthening too, hardening and clarifying themselves.

No wonder those primitive little dingoes had been missing during most of the party in Bungalow 10. While Burny had played his guitar and she had sambaed at the pool's edge with their charming host, his dogs had already been sent out across the woods to the point, deliberately loosed on another trial hunt that had brought them back to whine for reward at their master's ringed hand.

Had he known, then, that his "babies" had actually attacked Jan? Or at this stage of his derangement, had he only meant for them to further terrify the lone girl in the cabin?

Instead, they had succeeded in making one kill—a helpless kitten—and from the evidence of the black satin and the bloodstains, they must have injured Jan too, even horribly, when she finally made her dash for the security of the boat.

At least Jan had reached it, because it was gone. But what then? Jan had never been any good at handling fast boats. She could have overturned or piled herself up on the island's hazardous shore line. If she was bleeding badly or in hysterics— And the island itself was lightless, pathless.

Let her remember there's a cove where we used to picnic as kids. Dear God, let her be there, Laura prayed suddenly.

The prayer became a chant, matching the thrust of fear that drove her leg and arm muscles to a pace that was slowly devouring the distance still to go. . . .

Faltering with weariness, Laura finally had to drop her legs down and tread water. There were even moments now when she forgot why she swam.

She was in much colder water too, fed by springs. But at least the fragment of moon hung higher now, comforting her with its clearer light and enveloping the whole island in a silvered mist of energy.

She could see the cliff quite plainly at last, rising like a wall with only that deeply crumbled wedge to mar its face of stone. The cove was less than

172

fifty yards beyond, but it might as well have been five thousand.

Water plunked softly in hidden hollows, like some weird imitation of Burny's guitar, and she kicked out with the violence of self-preservation. She had seen more than one swimmer lose control in deep water. It was fatally easy to do. Added to the slow poison of fatigue, a swimmer could begin to imagine things. For instance, the impression that a boat was following her. That it had been for minutes.

She put out a weary arm and tried to swing her body around. Hope lifted through her. There *was* a boat. But the almost inaudible throb of its motor was coming from far behind her, from back near the point, which meant that it couldn't be Jan.

Hope died like a wet flare. A fisherman, probably, returning with a night's catch. Or some pre-dawn enthusiast just starting out, traveling quietly and slow, with due regard for the flightiness of fish.

Yet the boat was coming closer, instinct told her. And on the lift of uncertain fear, she began to swim hard again, using her last drive of endurance to reach the cove.

She collapsed onto the sand and had to labor for breath while she scanned the campsite, the pale line of the cove, the solid little dock that Gil had carpentered—all of them deserted beneath the moon.

There was no sign that her red outboard had ever reached the cove. No sign of Jan anywhere.

Defeat was a blow, followed by a disappointment so deep and harsh that the need finally broke through into full consciousness: She had wanted to find Gil here.

Was that so impossible? After leaving her with that brief kiss of farewell to seal their personal fiasco, Gil must have gone on to pick up Burny at Bungalow 10. Surely there had been time for them both to return here to their camp for the night. *And I wouldn't have expected anything but his help,* she thought.

Instead, a sound brushed her. It was like a light running at the edge of the woods. Like a soft crashing through underbrush. Shadows shifted, flecked with a queer double gleam of red. Then silence again, then the higher-up cascading of pebbles down a slope.

"Jan—? Jan!"

Laura stumbled to her own feet. But why should Jan be trying to reach the cliff? Because she was lost? Confused? Driven to seek the one high and open spot of vantage where she could see or be seen by someone?

Laura shouted her sister's name twice more, shattering a silence that seemed even more ominous once the echoes had died.

There was a lantern on the camp table. Somehow she found matches, and struck them repeatedly until the wick caught. Encased in the feeble glow, she finally broke her way through to the tracing of the path that circled upward.

Stumbling toward the rise, skinned on both knees and still clutching the lantern, she could see the open stars and the ledge of stone above her.

Once again it reached her—that sound of light running. Twigs broke to left and right behind her now. And there was the padding of feet, circling just beyond the safety of the lantern.

She must have whirled in confusion, because the lantern crashed against a tree and went out. She felt her eyes staring through the moonlight. There was blood on her leg; the shattering glass must have cut her.

Some other animals must have gotten onto the island, she decided. Not the dingoes. Not unless their master was with them.

She seemed to see his pale eyes and the shining chains he held and the smile of the crazed hunter. Then she heard herself screaming through her own fingers.

She heard a crashing on the path below her, followed by the rush of a man's body. He was breathing thickly as he reached for her. Then his hand came hard over her mouth, shutting off both sound and air.

Chapter Seventeen

The man who was holding her had a dark face, taut as a drum in the shifting moonlight, and the squarest shoulders she had ever clutched.

"Gil—?" she sobbed.

"Take it easy, honey. I had to stop you. You were screaming."

"But the dogs—!"

He froze. The word broke from him like a groan: "When?"

"I—I don't know. A few minutes ago. Earlier too!"

"Where?"

"I heard them down by the cove first. I thought it was Jan. Then on the path. Below me. All around!"

"Then let's go. Up," Gil ordered. "We're sitting ducks here in the woods."

Scrambling and half dragging her, Gil forced a swift climb to the bare ledge of rock that overhung the lake.

"Watch it," he had to bark or she might have gone on stumbling to the broken crevice.

"Gil!"

"Take it easy, Laura," he said quietly again. "Maybe they won't come back. If they do, you can dive for it, can't you?"

"Can you?"

"Sure. A backward one-and-a-half. We'll hold hands."

"But they're after Jan!"

"Not this time. They're trailing me. I really tore it tonight. It was worth it, too. You should have seen Harry's face! I was expecting to get jumped, but not this soon. I thought I could get you off the island."

"But the dingoes *are* after Jan," she insisted hysterically. "You don't understand. They've attacked her once already—back at the cabin. She got away, but she must be hurt. She left a note—"

"Which we read. How do you think we knew where to find you? We stumbled over that poor dead kitten; then we found her note, then your clothes. High heels, dress on the floor—just as if you'd stepped out of them fast. It wasn't hard to figure what had happened. No boat, so you swam after her. I said you'd make for the cove. Or maybe I just prayed that part."

"Who's we?" she asked thickly.

"Burny. He's got the speedboat. He dropped me off, then went on to search the shore line."

"But Burny's blind!"

"Try to get hold of yourself, will you? You know Burny can see. He's really had his eyes opened tonight! So have I. If Jan's afloat, he'll find her. And when he comes past here again, you dive. Just dive, get it? Not argue."

She wrung her hands. She started to babble at him.

"You don't understand," Gil said, driven finally to anger and hoarseness. "But me—I was supposed to carry around my own crystal ball! You've given me one devil of a bad time, do you realize that? So just be quiet for a minute. I want to remember if it was worth it."

Remember? His kiss brought sanity with it, quieting.

"Miss Nobility," Gil said against her trembling mouth. "Giving me all that talk about changing your mind and going away with Lasher. Wanting a career. Wanting anything he could give you. I almost believed you, too. Two of a kind. 'Sisters!' I thought. 'A pair of gentle little betrayers.' Then I saw his dogs."

"When?"

"When I went to pick up Burny after the party. And don't get careful with me, Laura. You'd found out who Lasher was and made a deal with him to let your sister alone. And me along with her."

"Did he tell you that?"

"*I* told me that. Up here." Gil tapped his forehead. "The minute I walked into his bungalow and saw those ugly little brutes, I recognized the breed. Australian dingoes? I told you once I'd tried to raise chickens down there. I've been all through the bush country. Then the other name for the breed suddenly clicked—warrigals—and the whole picture went clear.

"I told Burny to play something sweet while I had a talk with Mr. Big. A few people were still hanging around, drinking his liquor, but they looked harmless. I found him by the pool. I suggested that his real name was Harry Warrigal, that he had a bad reputation, and that decent people wouldn't give him the time of day if they knew what he was like.

"He was very polite. He said, 'You'd better get lost while you still can. And take Blind Boy with you.'

"I said I was as big a coward as the next guy but if he ever came anywhere near you again, I'd find a way not to care what he tried.

"He swore for a while. Then he said, 'You're lucky, Bricker. I'm going to forget the past and let you keep the blonde one after all. You can even finance a fling on the money she stole from me. I always did prefer them dark and beautiful.'

"So then I hit him. I used all I had, but he got up smiling. He said, 'You're dead, Bricker. This time it won't be nice, either.'

"There didn't seem to be any use standing around arguing the point, so I hustled Burny back down to the dock and we grabbed a boat. All I could think of was getting back to you. All I wanted to do was shake you. Trying to act noble and self-sacrificing when a psycho like that was calling the plays!"

"I didn't know what else to do," Laura mumbled.

"You could have told me who he was."

"And get you killed?"

"I do those little things for myself," Gil said.

He was growing quieter, more taut. She knew why he was talking so much too, why he stirred her closer to him on the uncomfortable rock.

With the dogs alerted for a kill and still prowling the woods, Gil wouldn't risk taking her down. If Burny came by with the boat, Gil would make her go off the cliff. If nothing happened, they'd wait for daylight.

"What happened next?" Laura asked, sweeping her eyes across the lake. "Keep talking, Gil. It's better when you talk."

"Well, by that time, Burny had taken off his glasses," Gil continued dryly. "He'd shoved them into his pocket and brought out some temper. He wanted to know what I was trying to do, taking a sock at Lasher—show off my muscles or wreck your career?

"I said, 'Wreck your career?' I said there'd be no career at all unless you wanted to handicap it with a husband who'd be playing the piano right behind you. With a real touchy style, too."

Gil paused, a deep crease in his forehead. "To tell you the truth, I was afraid I'd brought him on too fast. He just sat beside me in the boat, slumped a bit, nursing that guitar like it was his last friend. Then suddenly he twanged a sour chord and said, 'You'd better fill me in, man. I'm lost.'"

"Did you?" she asked.

"All the way. Everything," Gil nodded.

He was hefting a rock, half of his mind struggling with a problem which she didn't want to think about either. The rock was big, but somehow it didn't look big enough. At least Gil could move fast if he had to, up here in the open. And she could dive if the dogs came. She wouldn't, though. Not without him.

She heard Gil saying rather tonelessly, "I filled Burny in all the way back to that night-club date when we both got mixed up with Jan. I told him that he'd landed in the hospital by mistake—instead of me—because I'd been involved with her myself and this other character named Warrigal hadn't liked it. I explained to Burny why I'd brought him here to Talisman Lake—because I thought maybe I could locate Jan and make her go back to him; because *I* felt so guilty. Then I admitted hounding you into going to work on his morale and then trying to leave you holding the bag.

"I don't think I whitewashed it. Burny called me some choice names that fit. But the part that rocked him was that you and Jan were sisters and that you'd been letting her stay in your cabin all the time.

" 'Sisters!' he kept yelping. 'How could they be sisters?' "

" 'How could that polished maniac be Harry Warrigal?' I yelped right back. 'How could I operate so long with half a brain?' "

" 'Less than half,' he said. 'And blind. Blinder than you-know-who.' Then he said, 'I must have been sick in the head, Gil. But at least I've got talent. All you've got is trouble.' "

After a straining pause, Gil said, "He should have played it in B-flat. When we found that dead kitten, I knew what he meant. Then when I realized you were gone——"

Huddled against him, she heard herself mumble, "I don't know why they had to kill Phut-Phat. He was so little, Gil. Just a baby cat with blue eyes. He wasn't to blame for anything. The rest of us were, but not him."

"Were we? I wonder," Gil said, stroking the long black hair that covered her bare shoulders like a shroud. "How do things get started, anyway? It's like a machine rolling downhill. People get caught in the gears, and who do you blame? Even those dingoes—they didn't train themselves. I bet they'e be happier back in the bush country, hunting rabbits."

They moved together and kissed again.

"I love you, Laura. This is some place to have to say it though."

She clung to him and whispered back the immemorial words.

But the waiting was punishment. The broken cliff was like a platform hung in space. Not even a bird wing violated the silence of the woods below them.

"Maybe they've given up," Gil said at last, relief in his voice. "Maybe I can take you down—"

The color of the lake was changing, and the sky had lightened. There was a sweet and sudden stirring of life across the whole island.

"Why cry?" Gil said, touching the tears on her cheek. "We've come a long way, honey, and found some truth. And look—daylight. I think we're going to get lucky at last."

"Think again, piano player," said the man on the other side of the paling cliff. "And get her up. I want her to see this. I want her to see it good."

Harrison Lasher was still in gray, but he was immaculate. He must have come up over the other side of the cliff, beyond the broken crevice, and he was holding the whining dingoes on a pair of short bright chains that were curbed around the hand with the huge ring. His right arm cradled death.

Laura looked into the dull eye of the rifle and said, "Please let him alone. Please. I'll go with you right now. I'll do anything you want me to do. *Now*. Anything you say."

"You'll do that anyway," came the answer.

"If you touch her," Gil said, "I'll kill you. I don't know how, but I'm giving you the word."

His knuckles were still wrapped around the rock, but it must have shrunk. It looked like a pebble.

"A big mouth on a small talent," Lasher said. "Why didn't you play it smart, Bricker? Why did you have to hit me? Nobody hits me, and especially not you. I said you were welcome to the blonde. Now it looks like I get to manage both sides of the family!"

"Shut up!" Gil said.

He jiggled out a laugh while his dogs lunged at their chains, teeth bared and hackles rising. They were in a slavering fury of eagerness. Under their dancing paws, the pebbles cascaded over the brink like hail. "Tsk. Tsk. Not till I give the word, babies," Lasher said gleefully.

"What are you?" Gil said. "Human?"

Laura said, "You sound as if you'd rehearsed all this, Harry. Why don't you tell us all about it? That ought to give you more kicks. What do you do with the rifle? Fan yourself?"

"Attagirl!" Gil breathed.

"With the rifle, I perform a little 'accident,'" Harry answered in a pleasant tone. "A sad accident. You see, when I come upon this gentleman who's being practically mauled to death by my dogs, naturally I'm appalled. I try to drag them off, but it's impossible. I raise my rifle to shoot them, but I'm so shaken, my aim is poor. Unfortunately I miss the poor brutes and hit your piano player instead. But then hunting accidents happen all the time. Especially to people who shouldn't live."

Smiling, he wrapped the dogs' chains around his hand so that he could use the tip of the rifle to scratch the ears of Djong, who was twitching in a fury of eagerness. The growling of the other was as soft as the purr of an outboard that was certainly coming closer along the eastern shoreline.

Laura heard it, and then Gil heard it. The impact of his look almost made her obey him.

That's Burny, so dive! it ordered. Gil's eyes were curiously angry and stricken; yet he gave her one of those brief smiles. *Dive!*

She couldn't. How much did he expect of her? She moved beside him, where it was better, much better. She felt the convulsive grip of his fingers. It wasn't so difficult to face things together. She wondered why they couldn't have learned that sooner. She must have had a puzzled little smile on her own face when it happened.

She heard that jiggling laugh as Harry opened his hand like a man bestowing bounty, followed by the metallic rip on chain as the dogs lunged. She saw their fierce leap to clear the crevice. She even saw the body of the man in gray suddenly whip itself forward and back in a desperate lurch for equilibrium, like a skier's body caught off balance against the pale flush of dawn.

He was there and then he was nowhere.

Was there a scream? Not until he hit the water.

Then, for seconds again, there was only the cascade of pebbles over the brink after him, mixed with the agitated whining of the dingoes as they raced back and forth at the cliff's edge in a panic for their master's safety.

"What happened?" a voice inquired. It sounded like her own.

"The chains must have caught on his ring," Gil said slowly. "When the dogs lunged, it was like being hitched to a rocket."

Djong was barking frantically at the flailing arms far below him. Suddenly he flattened his front legs for the slide into space. He launched himself over the edge first, followed by Wallah, his pitifully helping mate.

They hit the surface on their bellies and came up like a pair of corks, front paws pumping madly to the rescue. The man in the water screamed and went under again.

Staring down, Laura said, "He can't swim."

"What?"

"He wanted me to give him lessons."

"Are you crazy?" Gil cried.

"He can't swim, but I can," she whispered.

"Do you know what that man is? The things he's done? Not just to us but—!"

"For once there's a choice. If we just let him drown—afterwards—when we look at each other, what do we call it?"

And Gil swore, his face stained with exhaustion, his eyes as cold as an executioner's.

"Do we call it murder?" she said. "Or just an accident we let happen to someone who shouldn't live?"

They stood like guilty conspirators, gazing down at the desperate little animals paddling with piston feet toward the spot where their master was choking and sobbing like a crazed child.

She heard Gil's violent intake of breath.

"God. O.K.!" he exploded in the ultimate of fury as he ripped off his shirt. "But this is my bit."

"Haven't you learned anything?" she asked him, calculating their dive. "There's no bottom down there, Gil. We're going together."

Chapter Eighteen

It was a beautiful dive, Laura realized in that split-second when she and Gil sailed through the light air of daybreak.

The water was a pearl pink now, and they hit it with a precision that brought them up parallel and let them do the next twenty yards at a driving pace.

But the frantic dingoes had reached their master first.

Barking with joy, they scratched at his flailing arms and tried to help by climbing onto his head. When he grabbed at them, screaming thickly with water in his throat, they bit at him in an agony of excitement. And when they had forced him under and he didn't come up, they swam around in circles of bewilderment.

Gil dove again and again, his face as grim as a savage. He and Laura even spelled each other, working a cross pattern that might have reached bottom if there had been a bottom. But even ten feet down, the water was viciously cold, fed by the unsounded springs.

"It's no use," Gil gasped at last, grabbing her as

she readied for another surface dive. They clung together, exhausted.

Even the dogs seemed to know that it was hopeless. Like a pair of water-logged mourners, they had turned their noses toward the cove and were paddling sadly away when Burny pulled up in the slowly revving outboard.

There was nothing the matter with his eyesight now. Burny reached down a bony hand for Gil and then together, they managed to haul Laura over the side.

It was her own boat. And there were two sisters aboard. Unable to get her chattering teeth apart, Laura felt Gil throw a towel around her blue shoulders. On the back seat, covered with another beach towel and shreds of her black silk dress, Jan seemed to be snoring into her spun-gold hair.

"What happened?" Gil barked.

"Complete exhaustion. It's a beautiful anaesthetic," Burny murmured, spinning the wheel like a professional.

"Is she hurt?" Laura gasped.

"Clawed pretty bad on the legs. We'd better get her to a doctor. I found her stuck in the shallows by the old pier. Luckily she was too afraid to climb out. She started to cry and then babble at me. She said she'd had the kitten in her arms when she ran from the cabin. It got scared and jumped, and the dogs stopped to tear it apart. That's what gave her time to reach the boat. Then she blacked out on me again. I couldn't wake her up. I used to be crazy about her, remember? I may even decide I still am, once she wakes up again."

"All right, but let's go," Gil said. "We've got to get to a phone."

"Trouble?" Burny asked more quietly.

"We need the sheriff. Harry Warrigal's dead."

"Did you kill him?" Burny suggested as he set a straight course for Lee's Landing.

"His own dogs killed him. They drowned him."

"Well, that seems about fair," Burny said.

Gil's arm was lying heavily across her shoulder, and Laura realized that his dark gaze was fixed on Spider Island. It seemed to be swimming on a sea of gold.

She said, "Do you want to go back someday?"

"Do you?"

"It's still mine. Perhaps just the two of us—"

"It's an idea."

"Oh, Gil—do you mean that?" she whispered.

"Well, we could start with one cabin," his tired voice said. "We might even wind up running our own resort. I'd like that, and why not?"

"Money?" Burny said. "Money comes high these days."

"So I finish out our contract here, and then I go to work. I mean, real work."

"And I can always sing," Laura suggested without any spirit.

"Not with me, you can't," Burny said. "I've just about had it with you two. And Lohengrin's not my kind of Jazz. I think I'll play it solo from now on. A real cool solo on a lonesome beat."

"I'm sorry, Burny—" and Gil's frown was troubled. "She just comes first with me. She always should have. I know we've been together a long time—"

"Too long. You should have kicked me out of the nest when I first began to squawk."

"No hard feelings?"

"I'll teach your first kid to play the guitar."

Above the thin cheekbones, Burny's eyes were the color of blue smoke. The blue smoke of genius, Laura thought, that would drift through a thousand jazz sessions, a thousand intensities, a thousand more problems.

Impulsively she slid her hand beneath Burny's on the wheel and felt him squeeze it and give it back to her so that she could put it where it belonged. In Gil's square grip.

There was just a chance that even Jan might wake up a little wiser. *This might just be the beginning of a pretty good beginning,* she thought wearily.

Only the daylight was too clear. Laura closed her eyes and snuggled down sleepily between the only two men she had ever loved.